DALE
EARNHARDT

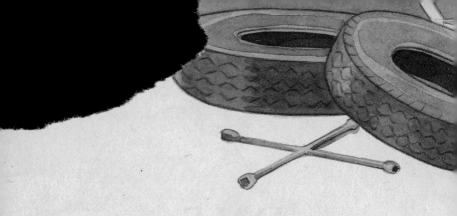

Illustrated by Meryl Henderson

DALE EARNHARDT
Young Race Car Driver

by Paul Mantell

ALADDIN PAPERBACKS

New York   London   Toronto   Sydney

❦

ALADDIN PAPERBACKS
An imprint of Simon & Schuster
Children's Publishing Division
1230 Avenue of the Americas
New York, NY 10020
Text copyright © 2006 by Paul Mantell
Illustrations copyright © 2006 by Meryl Henderson
All rights reserved, including the right of
reproduction in whole or in part in any form.
ALADDIN PAPERBACKS, CHILDHOOD OF FAMOUS AMERICANS,
and colophon are trademarks of Simon & Schuster, Inc.
Designed by Lisa Vega
The text of this book was set in New Caledonia.
Manufactured in the United States of America
First Aladdin Paperbacks edition October 2006
2 4 6 8 10 9 7 5 3 1
Library of Congress Control Number: 2006923542
ISBN-13: 978-1-4169-1266-8
ISBN-10: 1-4169-1266-5

ILLUSTRATIONS

CONTENTS

Prologue:
1951

The noise in the mill was deafening. The big machines rolled on and on, and cotton dust filled the air. Ralph Earnhardt coughed it out—but some of the tiny fibers stayed stuck inside his lungs. Some always did.

Cotton dust was evil stuff. But if you didn't have a high school diploma—and Ralph didn't—work in the Cannon Mills was just about the only way there was to make a living in the tiny town of Kannapolis, North Carolina. It was the only way to feed your family.

Family. Ralph whispered the word. Tonight, his family would grow by one. His wife was having their third child! And here he was, stuck in the mill till six o'clock.

Ralph looked around at the dismal factory building. Would this be his children's fate too? Slaving away here for a poor man's wage while other folks got rich?

Finally, the bell clanged, signaling the change of shifts. Ralph elbowed his fellow workers aside, shoving his way through. His eyes were fixed on the exit doors, and he paid no attention to anyone else. He shot through gaps in the crowd, just like he did in his car at the Saturday night races.

Today he was in a big hurry to get home. He ran practically the whole way until he reached Car Town, the neighborhood where he lived, and turned the corner onto Coach Street.

He could see the midwife's car, still parked in front of their apartment house. She'd been

2

there since before he'd left for work that morning, helping Martha with her labor. He sure would have thought she'd be gone by now.

Unless . . . unless something was wrong.

He yanked open the apartment door and yelled, "Martha? Martha, are you all right?"

The midwife, an elderly lady, came out of the bedroom, wiping her hands dry with a towel and smiling. "It's all right, Mr. Earnhardt. It took a long time, but the baby came out fine."

Ralph breathed a sigh of relief. "And Martha?"

"She's fine too. Tired, but happy."

"And the baby . . . it's . . . ?"

"Oh! It's a boy. Congratulations."

"Thank you."

A son!

A little brother for Kaye and Kathy.

"Would you like to go in now and see them?"

The midwife ushered him into the bedroom. Then she backed out the door, closing it behind her, and leaving the three of them alone together—father, mother, and new baby.

Martha lay in the bed, smiling up at him, holding the gurgling infant in her arms. *Their son.*

"Hello, Ralph," she said in an exhausted voice.

Ralph smiled. "My, my, my."

After that, he didn't know what to say or do. He just stood there, like a tree, swaying back and forth, and staring at his wife and son.

Finally, Martha took pity on him. With a short laugh, she held the baby up. "You want to hug him?" she asked.

Ralph blinked, and bit his lip. "Uh . . . maybe I'd better not. . . ."

She laughed again. "It's all right. He won't break."

"What if I drop him?"

"You won't. You're the most sure-handed man I've ever known. Why, look at the way you handle that race car of yours."

It was true—he did handle a car as well as anyone. If he could ever make enough money at racing, maybe someday he could quit the mill.

Trouble was, you had to be racing nearly every night if you hoped to win enough money to support a family. And if you didn't win, how were you going to pay the rent and put food on the table?

Even if you did win, on any given night you took home only a couple hundred dollars. Half that much for second, even less for third. Fourth place, you got nothing—not one cent for all your time, gas, and trouble.

It was no way to support a wife and children.

Ralph took the baby in his arms. The child was snugly wrapped in a blanket, even though it was warm for the end of April. "Hello, little man," he said, nuzzling the baby's soft skin with his grizzled cheek. "Little Ralph Jr."

"Oh, Ralph," said Martha, frowning. "It's gonna be so confusing with you both having the same name."

"Let's just call him Junior then."

"Junior? Why can't he have a name all his own?"

Ralph frowned, thinking about it. "How 'bout we call him by his middle name—Dale?"

Martha smiled, closing her eyes. "Dale. Yes, I like that. I'll just call him Dale."

Ralph put his lips to the baby's ear and whispered. "Junior? This is your daddy talking to you. I want you to get one thing straight right off the bat. You listening?"

The baby stared at him, his eyes wide open, and made a cooing baby noise.

"Good," Ralph said. "Just remember this—you're gonna grow up and finish high school, understand? You're gonna get a good education, and you're gonna get that diploma, and you're gonna get someplace in life . . . not like your daddy. There. Now I've said my piece."

He gave the baby back to Martha. "I'll let y'all sleep now," he said, and went out of the room. "G'night, Martha. G'night . . . Junior."

The Will to Win
1957–1958

"Is that your go-kart, Dale?"

"Uh-huh." Dale saw Jimmy standing in the doorway of the garage, and stood up to face his friend from first grade. "My daddy built it for me. I'm gonna race it Saturday, and I'm gonna win, too. This baby's fast." He patted his brand-new go-kart, careful not to touch any of the wet paint.

The big cinder-block garage doubled as Ralph Earnhardt's shop. He'd built it himself, so he'd have a place to put together his race cars. He built them from scratch—picking up parts at local junk yards and body shops.

Dale loved hanging out in the shop. Even when he was just a little kid of two or three, he'd sit on the cement floor, racing his toy cars, going "Vroom! Vroom!" while his daddy worked underneath his latest ride.

"My cousin Ernie's got a go-kart too," said Jimmy. "He's seven. And he says *he's* gonna win that race."

"Oh, yeah? Well, he's wrong," said Dale. "Cause *I'm* gonna win it. Can't both of us win. So you tell him from me, he's gonna lose."

Jimmy grinned, then pointed over to Ralph Earnhardt's grown-up–sized racing car, hiked up on jacks over on the other side of the shop. "Your daddy build that car too?"

"Yup," said Dale, squinting hard at his friend. "You can look at it, but don't you touch it."

"You ever touched it?"

"Sure I have. Plenty of times. My daddy lets me wash it, change the oil, and everything."

9

Jimmy went over to the sleek black car. He walked all around it, taking in every detail. On top of the windshield the words GO OR BLOW were painted in white. On the driver-side door, over the number 8, it said RALPH.

Dale watched him carefully, making sure his friend didn't touch anything.

There were other signs painted on the car too. On the rear door it said EDELMAN'S GARAGE, CARSON BLVD., KANNAPOLIS. On the front right fender, it said DAINTY MAID FOOD PRODUCTS. Jimmy slowly sounded the names out.

Dale wished he could read as well as Jimmy, but hey—they were only in first grade. He'd get the hang of reading sooner or later.

"Why's it say those things, Dale?"

"What things?"

"Like Edelman's Garage."

"Mr. Edelman gave my daddy some parts for free," Dale explained. "That's called a sponsor."

There. Now he was smarter than Jimmy,

11

telling him a thing or two he didn't know.

"Man," Jimmy said, "I'd like to drive one of these babies someday."

Dale could tell Jimmy wanted to touch the car. He walked over there and stood beside him—just to make sure he didn't sneak a hand over. "I'm gonna drive it as soon as I'm old enough," he told his friend. "I'm gonna race it. And I'm gonna win, too. Just like I'm gonna win that go-kart race on Saturday."

The other boy frowned. "You always win. At everything."

Dale felt his chest swell with pride. "I don't like losing."

Jimmy made a face. "How'd you learn to ride a bike backward?"

"I'm not telling," Dale said.

"Aw, come on! Teach me!"

"I don't know how I learned it. I just . . . did."

Jimmy was mad now. "I can still ride a bike faster than you," he muttered.

"Can't either."

"Can too."

"Can not!"

"Race you down to the general store."

"I'm just painting my go-kart here," Dale protested. "I've got no time to—"

"I'm goin' then," said Jimmy. "If I get there first, you lose."

Dale threw down the paint brush. "You ain't gettin there first," he said, and ran outside to get his bike.

Down the driveway they raced, side by side, and turned onto Sedan Avenue. Dale turned wide, making his friend swerve onto the sidewalk. Jimmy had to put one leg down to keep from crashing into somebody's fence.

Dale, meanwhile, was pedaling furiously, already halfway down the block.

"HEY!" Jimmy called out behind him. "That's no fair!"

Dale kept pedaling away. "I ain't losing," he said under his breath.

School was hard for Dale. Sitting there at a desk, hour after hour, while the teacher went on about things Dale didn't care a hoot about. He kept fidgeting and staring out the window. He wished he were outside, in the fine weather, racing bikes or go-karts.

Tomorrow was Saturday. He would go to Columbia, South Carolina, with his daddy, his momma, and his brothers and sisters to watch "Ironheart" race at the speedway.

"Ironheart"—that was his daddy's nickname. It sounded like Earnhardt, but it meant his daddy was the best driver of them all.

The only thing better than hanging around his daddy's shop, watching him work on cars, was going to the dirt tracks and watching him race.

Tomorrow would be a good day. It might even be a great day if his daddy won.

His daddy won lots of times. Other times, he came in second or third—good enough to make money at it.

14

Dale loved to hang around the shop out back and watch his daddy work. Ralph Earnhardt would get a late-model car, take it apart, and put it back together again, fine-tuned with special parts.

Sometimes other grown-ups would come by to watch. They'd offer advice, but Ralph just nodded, not saying if he thought the advice was good. Nobody knew how to fix up a car and make it run fast better than he did.

The other drivers at the short tracks called "bull rings"—because the crowds were right on top of the action, just as in bull fighting—were afraid of his daddy. Dale knew it. He saw that look in their eyes when the Earnhardt family's truck showed up at a track, towing the race car behind it. They looked *scared*. "Uh-oh, bad news," they were thinking. "Ironheart's here."

Sitting in class now, Dale could still feel the excitement of race time the weekend before, when the starter's voice came on the loudspeakers, saying, "Gentlemen, start your engines!"

Then all the drivers flicked their switches at once, and the roaring noise of forty racing engines was enough to make you deaf.

All the cars were lined up along the straight-away in order of how fast they'd qualified. Fastest went first, on the inside row. That was called "pole position," the best place to start a race.

Lined up in two rows, inside and outside, all the cars rode around the track a few times, behind the pace car, which was out there only to set the pace.

When the drivers were all in the right positions, the starter would wave his green flag, the pace car would drive off the track into pit row (where cars went to change tires and gas up), and the race would be on.

The roar really got loud then! Red dirt would fly everywhere—mud, if it was raining—and the cars would race around the oval, trying to pass each other.

That year, Ralph Earnhardt was leading in points for the NASCAR (National Association for Stock Car Auto Racing) Late Model Sportsman Division Championship. Dale had told all the other boys what this meant—that his daddy was the best driver in the world.

But when he told his daddy what he'd said, Ralph replied, "That's not true, boy. There are whole other racing circuits, where drivers drive on asphalt tracks, with real expensive cars. They go much faster'n the cars I drive. And there's real prize money—not the chicken feed they give us for winning."

"Well, then, why don't you drive those other cars?" Dale asked.

"It ain't that simple," Ralph replied. "You need money. Lots of money."

"How much?"

"Millions. Gotta get big companies to back you and be your sponsors—like Ford and

Chevy—to put you in that expensive car and pay a whole crew to work on it. The driver doesn't work on the car like I do. He just drives. You've gotta have a whole team to race—not just one man, like me."

"You're not just a one-man team, Daddy," Dale said. "You've got me—we've got a two-man team!"

That made Ralph Earnhardt smile. He ruffled Dale's hair. "That's right, boy. It's you and me. But these teams have got six or seven people to build the car, and they've got pit crews with fancy uniforms who keep it going during the race. All I've got for my pit crew is Uncle Dub."

Uncle Dub was the man who came to races with Ralph and worked the pit for him. He wasn't really Dale's uncle, even though he knew to call him that.

"Those teams even have extra cars, in case one wrecks or goes bad," Ralph went on. "Yeah, it takes lots of money. Lots more'n

18

I've got. That's why I'm still just a plain old lint head."

That was what they called the workers at the fabric mill—lint heads—because they were always full of lint from the cotton.

It was a bad name to call someone, Dale knew. He wished his daddy wouldn't call himself such a bad name.

"If I'd stayed in school and gotten my high school diploma, instead of dropping out in the sixth grade to support my family, there's no telling what I could've been," Ralph said. "And that's why you've got to do well in school, Dale. You've got to get a high school diploma, so you won't wind up a grease monkey or a lint head like me."

"Why don't you just quit working at that mill?" Dale asked him once. "You could make enough prize money racing. You could get a big sponsor and race on those asphalt tracks. You're the best driver there is."

But his daddy didn't answer him. He just

stared into space until Dale got tired of waiting and went back into the house.

One night at the Columbia Speedway, Dale watched his daddy go from twenty-fifth place all the way to first, bumping other cars right out of the way one after the other. Some got spun around, then managed to get back into the race. Others blew a tire or hit the wall, and had to quit.

He thought the other drivers must be mad about it.

Sure enough, one of the other drivers came over to Ralph Earnhardt's car and kicked a dent in the fender. "There!" the angry driver said. "Now you can use your prize money to fix your own car! See how you like it!"

Dale thought his father would get out of the car and whup the other man. But Ralph just sat there, saying, "That's racing, man."

"Like fun it is!" the other man said, and gave the fender another kick before storming off.

"Why didn't you bust him one, Daddy?" Dale asked as his father got out of the car.

"I didn't know if he had a knife or a gun or whatever," Ralph explained. "Dale, there's no use getting into fights with people. You do whatever you've got to do to win on the track. *That's* the time to prove you're a man. Then afterward, you leave it all behind you. I've got nothing to prove to anybody—except out *there*."

It was a moment Dale would always remember. There would be many lessons like that. His daddy didn't usually say much, but when he did, it was mostly worth remembering.

Dale knew his daddy loved him, and was saying so in those few words of wisdom, even if Ralph never said it directly.

After school most days Dale practically ran home, tossed his books in the house, and headed out around back to the oversize garage that housed his dad's shop. When his dad wasn't on shift at the mill, he was usually here, working on his race car.

Ralph never said much in the garage, and neither did Dale. But the two of them understood each other. They were alike in so many ways—but different, too.

"You do your homework today?" Ralph would ask him.

"Not yet."

"Get in the house and do it then."

"I'll do it later."

"You'll do it now."

"I can't think straight right after school, Daddy. I need some time to relax."

His father looked him over, then tossed him a wrench to clean. "All right, son," he said. "Just see that it gets done. Nothing's more important than school—remember that."

Dale didn't answer back. That would only have gotten him yelled at—but he wanted to argue with his dad. He hated being in school, and he didn't see what was so important about it.

School would never be as important to him as cars—even if it meant he became a lint head like his daddy. Dale didn't care what happened to him, so long as he could race cars someday.

Racing was all he cared about. Whenever he wasn't in school or helping his daddy in the shop, Dale would be building model cars, or racing slot cars, or building and racing bikes and go-karts.

When he was with his friends, he liked to brag about how he knew everything there was to know about cars, and how to fix them and race them. That kind of talk impressed the other boys, and it made Dale feel like somebody special.

But he would never dare talk like that around his daddy. His daddy would never put up with him bragging. He'd put Dale in his place, just like that.

Ralph Earnhardt was tough. So over time Dale learned to act tough too. To him, it was how a man acted. If he hurt himself with a wrench or a screwdriver, he didn't cry. He just kept quiet and waited for his daddy to tell him he'd done well.

Ralph did praise Dale . . . once in a while. Not very often, though.

Dale would tighten the lug nuts on the tires so tight he'd nearly bust a gut doing it. Then Ralph would look it over and ask, "You sure it's tight enough? 'Cause if it ain't, I might crash. You willing to have it be your fault if I do?"

And Dale would tighten the nut even tighter, until his hands were red and blistered from gripping the wrench so hard.

"That's the trouble with you, boy," his dad said as he struggled. "You don't try nearly hard enough."

"How can you say that?" Dale complained.

"You want proof? Look at the grades you get in school."

He had no answer for that one, but that

didn't stop him from being furious. He stared at his blistered hands and steamed.

One day, Dale promised himself, he'd show his daddy just how tough he was. Tougher even than the old man himself!

Wild Thing
1961

Dale had started to notice that his daddy was acting quieter than usual. Whole dinners would go by without him saying a word. You could hear the forks and knives tinkling in the dining room as the family ate.

Only the gurgles of the babies broke the painful silence. There were five children now—Kaye, Kathy, Dale, Randy, and Danny—five little mouths to feed.

Ralph was spending even more time than usual in the shop. He'd come home from the mill, go straight to the garage, and work till dinner. Then after his meal, he'd go right back out there and work some more.

Looking out his bedroom window before going to sleep, Dale could see the blowtorch blazing as his daddy welded something under the chassis (the frame of the car).

Then one evening after work, when they were all seated at the dinner table, Ralph dropped the bomb. "I quit work today," he said.

Martha Earnhardt dropped her fork and knife. They clattered on her plate, but she didn't seem to notice. "You quit?" she repeated.

"Uh-huh," Ralph said.

"Ralph Earnhardt, have you gone and lost your mind?"

"I'm sorry, Martha. I just couldn't take it anymore."

Dale's mother calmed herself down and considered this. "You gonna find yourself another job?"

"Nope. I'm gonna race the car full-time. There's dirt tracks in nearly every town in Carolina these days. Same thing all across the South. They've got races going on nearly every night of the week. I figure I can win twice as much racing full-time. If I do, I'll earn almost what I did at the mill."

"*If*." His mom patted her lips with a napkin. "But there's no guarantee. No paycheck in your pocket every week. You sure we're gonna be all right?"

Dale saw his father's jaw grow tight. "Don't you worry," he said. "We'll be all right. I'll see to it. If I can't do it without taking away from the family, I'll go back to the mill."

And that was that. From then on, his daddy didn't go to work at the mill. He took the car out racing three, four, even five nights a week.

Whenever Ralph was home in between races, he spent all day in the shop—and whenever Dale could, he made sure he was right there by his daddy's side, helping get the car ready for the next race.

Ralph built his own chassis and his own engines. He fussed over every nut and bolt, every hose and wire. He might not have the fastest car in any given race—but he'd have the sturdiest and best maintained one. He'd at least finish every race, even if he didn't win. No car of his would ever quit on him.

As he told Dale, "It isn't always the fastest car that wins the race. Lots of times, it's the best driver."

"And what makes the best driver, Daddy?" Dale asked.

Ralph looked him right in the eye. "I'll tell you one thing, boy," he said. "Whatever it is, they can't put it in you. But they can take it out."

The whole family went to the races on weekends. During the week they had to stay behind because of school.

On the day after his dad came back from a

race where the family hadn't joined him, Dale would run out first thing in the morning to see the car. He could tell how well his daddy had done the night before just by how much mud was on the front of it. A lot of mud meant Ralph had been in back of the pack. Not so much meant he'd run at the front—first or second probably.

Most times it was pretty clean. After all, his daddy was one of the best. Hadn't he won the Late Model Sportsman Division Championship back in '56?

Ralph Earnhardt was quickly developing a reputation as a great driver. Before he quit his job at the mill and started racing full-time, he'd only been known at the local tracks. Now, they knew about Ironheart all up and down the East Coast.

He won so much, and by such a margin, that people didn't want to buy tickets anymore. What was the point of spending money to see someone win so easily? For a few weeks certain tracks even banned him from racing.

Finally, Ralph figured out a way around the problem. He would lag back for most of the race, then take the lead only at the end, winning by just a little. "There's only one lap you need to lead," he told Dale, "and that's the last lap."

Dale didn't have to sit in the stands like everybody else. He got to watch the race from the back of the Earnhardts' truck.

His daddy would lie in wait, letting the other drivers make mistakes. Then, when they weren't paying attention, he'd pass them!

Lately, Ralph had started doing some driving on asphalt tracks, too—that's where the big money was. That February, he drove in the Daytona 500 in Florida, the biggest stock car race of them all.

Dale was sure his dad would win the big race—but he didn't. He didn't even finish in the money.

Great driver or not, with a second-rate car,

Ralph Earnhardt stood little chance against the best and most expensive cars in the race.

And there was no second chance afterward, either. No big company offered to sponsor him. No race team owner offered him another chance to drive at the big race.

Dale couldn't understand why. Wasn't Ironheart the best driver there was?

He asked his dad about it, but Ralph only said, "There's lots more drivers than there are teams, son. Besides, team owners want drivers who'll tow the line, and do everything they say. I guess I'm too independent for them."

But there was more to it than that. Dale had seen the way his dad had driven—so careful, not taking any big chances. What Dale didn't understand was *why*.

The truth was, even though the slogan on his regular car read GO OR BLOW, Ralph Earnhardt couldn't take the chance of going all out from the beginning of a race to the end.

He couldn't risk wrecking his only car—there would have been no money to replace it. And he certainly wasn't going to risk somebody else's car at the Daytona 500.

Maybe driving all out was what it would have taken for some big sponsor to notice him—but Ralph couldn't chance it. Even though he always made a living at racing from the day he quit the mill, he never did get his big break—never got the chance to race for the big prize money week after week.

It made Dale angry to see how his daddy, the world's greatest driver, was kept from reaching the top. He swore to himself that when it was his turn, he would do whatever it took to win the Daytona 500—even if he had to wreck every other car in the race to get there!

Over the years Dale had gotten pretty good at helping in the shop. Ralph had taught him how to change the oil, grease the wheels, clean the carburetor, and change the tires, the plugs, the shocks—almost anything that wasn't too complicated for a ten-year-old.

These were good times for Dale. He was spending more time with his father. Even better, he was learning more and more about cars. Pretty soon, he'd be able to take one apart and put it back together good as new all by himself.

Just like his daddy.

For Ralph Earnhardt, though, times were not as good. He was earning just about what he used to make at the mill—maybe even a little more. But it was never enough money to put away for a rainy day.

And when he had a bad week, he had to choose between giving Martha the money to buy food, or spending it on the repairs and upgrades that would help him win money in the next race.

Ralph always fed his family first. They never went hungry. As far as Dale and his brothers and sisters were concerned, the family wasn't poor—at least not any poorer than all the other families in Car Town whose fathers worked at the mill.

Still, things were tense around the house. Martha Earnhardt looked anxious and worried most of the time.

It wasn't just the money, either.

Car racing was a dangerous sport. Drivers got hurt all the time—once in a while, somebody even got killed. She knew it could happen to Ralph—but she also knew he loved to race. It was at the very heart of him, and she never tried to make him give it up.

But when Dale told her he wanted to grow up to be a race car driver, she told him to get that notion right out of his head. "It's much too dangerous," she said. "No son of mine is going to get himself killed just to win a few hundred dollars."

"Daddy does it."

"Your daddy's got racing in his soul, Dale.

I love him, but that's who he is, and I'd never try and change it. But you're my blood kin. You're a living, breathing part of me. It's different, how you feel about your children. Someday you'll understand."

Maybe. But from the time he'd been two or three years old—as far back as he could remember—Dale had known he wanted to be a race car driver like his daddy.

He could hardly wait till he was old enough to get behind the wheel of a car and drive himself.

He would go so fast, he would leave everyone in the dust behind him!

One day, when no one was looking, he went out into the driveway, got into his daddy's truck, and sat behind the wheel. He found that he couldn't see over the dashboard, so he borrowed a cushion from the living room sofa. He couldn't reach some of the pedals either—but a sturdy stick helped him hold the clutch down so he could switch gears.

He pretended to drive the truck, closing his eyes and imagining the road in front of him, turning the steering wheel back and forth, mock shifting in and out of gears.

Seeing his daddy coming out the back door of the house, he quickly got out of the truck's cab—but not quickly enough.

"What do you think you're doin'?" his father asked him.

"Nothin'."

"Nothin' my foot. You quit foolin' around with that truck, you hear?"

"Yes, Daddy."

"You ain't old enough to be driving. Not even pretend driving."

"I know how," Dale said.

"You think you know how. That ain't the same as knowing."

"Is so."

"Boy, are you arguing with me?"

Dale bit his lip. "No sir."

38

"'No sir' is right," said his father. "Now come on and help me change these tires." He went into the shop and knelt down beside the race car.

Dale didn't follow him. He could *so* drive!

His daddy didn't believe him, did he? Well, then, he'd just prove it to him once and for all!

Dale opened the door of the truck and swung himself back up into the driver's seat. Before Ralph Earnhardt even noticed what was happening, Dale started the engine, released the parking brake, and shifted into first gear.

"Hey!" he heard his daddy shouting from the garage. "What in the world are you doing?"

Dale couldn't help grinning—a crooked grin, just one corner of his mouth curling up. He saw his daddy in the rearview mirror, waving at him to stop. But it was too late. Dale was already rolling down the driveway and

onto Sedan Avenue. And he wasn't about to stop now.

In fact, he couldn't have stopped if he wanted to. In his eagerness to drive the truck, he'd forgotten to find a way to reach the brake pedal!

Bang! He hit one of their neighbors' garbage cans and knocked it over into the street!

As he turned onto the avenue, Dale caught one last glimpse of his daddy in the rearview mirror.

Ralph Earnhardt had both hands on his hips and was yelling something that Dale couldn't hear. He could see the proud, crooked grin on his daddy's face, though.

It matched his own perfectly.

Like father, like son.

A Flying Leap
1967

Ralph Earnhardt's one-man team had long ago become a two-man team, with Dale as his chief mechanic and all-around shadow. He even replaced Uncle Dub as Ralph's pit crew sometimes—whenever he could get off from school, that is.

It was getting harder and harder for Dale to keep plugging away—sitting behind a desk all day, then doing his homework after school—when all he wanted to do was work in the shop and follow his dad to the racetrack.

He was having more and more trouble paying attention to his teachers, and his grades were going from Cs to Ds, with a couple of Fs thrown in for good measure.

Twice already, he'd left ninth grade and quit school, only to have his dad scream his head off at him and make him go back and start over again. Dale was trying his best—well, some of the time—but it was just so hard to keep his mind on schoolwork!

They were at the Columbia Speedway one weekend. Dale had been there plenty of times before, but this day was special. He'd persuaded Pete Keller, one of the NASCAR officials who supervised the Sportsman Racing Circuit, to get him a rookie driver license.

Dale was only sixteen, but it wasn't like he was going to really get in a car and drive. The rookie license was just a pass to get him onto the infield in the middle of the track.

He fished a quarter out of his pocket, bought a hot dog, and ran out to the press truck. It was a big flatbed, parked smack in the middle of the oval.

This was where all the reporters who covered the Sportsman circuit watched the race. They would scribble on their notepads, then after the race, they'd hurry to the pressroom and type out their stories for the next day's papers.

Dale knew many of them, and they knew him by name. They'd joke around with him and the other drivers' kids, who were always chasing each other around the stands. But to let Dale join them in the press truck—that was a new one.

He leaned over the railing, watching the rookie drivers make their practice runs. This was where he wanted to be. This was paradise! He breathed in deeply, smelling the racing fuel and the cotton candy, the cigar smoke and burning rubber.

The rookie drivers raced around the oval, one after another, their engines roaring. Dale felt in his pocket for the rookie driver's license. He was one of them, and he had the pass to prove it!

Sure, it was just a dream—for now. But someday he'd be out there for real, driving a car of his own. Dale could hardly wait.

In fact, he couldn't wait at all.

Tomorrow he was going to have it out with his dad.

"Daddy?"

Ralph Earnhardt's hand reached out from under the car. "Hand me that number six screwdriver blade, son."

Dale got the blade and placed it in his father's hand.

"These Craftsman blades are better than the axle keys I've been using. The metal's harder—they won't break under pressure like the ones everybody's been using."

"I guess all the other drivers'll be doin' the same thing pretty soon," Dale said.

"Nope. I went down to Sears in Charlotte—that's the only place that sells them around here—and I bought up every number six screwdriver they had. That way, nobody else can steal my trick."

Dale filed this information away in the back of his brain. It was the kind of exciting detail he had no trouble remembering. If only it was that way with the stuff they taught in school!

But it wasn't.

"Daddy?" he said again.

"Just a minute," his father growled, annoyed.

Dale couldn't tell if his dad was mad at him or at the car. He heard Ralph grunting with the effort of making a screwdriver blade do something it wasn't made to do.

Finally, the grunting stopped, and his dad rolled out from under the car. Lying on his back on the dolly, he looked up at Dale and said, "What?"

"Um . . ."

"You tightened them lug nuts so tight I couldn't get 'em loose," his father complained.

"But you said—"

"Never mind that," Ralph Earnhardt interrupted, cutting him off. "We need to get these new axle keys put on before dinner."

Dale went over to the far wall and fetched another number six. "Daddy, I've got something to tell you."

"Well, let's hear it. We've got work to do."

"Now, don't be mad."

That got his father's attention. "Mad?" He frowned, got up off the dolly, and stood, his hands on his hips. "Boy, what did you go and do?"

"Nothin'!"

"Nothin'?"

"I . . . I quit school."

"*Again*?"

"I'm staying quit this time too. I've had

enough, Daddy. I tried hanging with it, but it's just too hard. I know you want me to finish high school, but there's no way. I'll never get through four years. I can't even get through another day!"

Ralph Earnhardt took this all in. For a long time—it seemed like hours—he just stared right through Dale. It was as if he were looking, not at his son, but at a reflection of himself as a young man.

He sighed deeply, shook his head, and said, "You're going back to school, son. You're gonna work your rear end off, and you're gonna pass your classes, and you're gonna get your diploma."

"I'm not," Dale insisted, holding his ground.

"I'm not giving you a choice."

"I'm not asking your permission."

"You're sixteen-years-old, boy. You don't know a thing about life. You want to wind up a lint head?"

"I won't," Dale said. "*You* quit the mill, didn't you?"

"I'm eleven thousand dollars in debt," his father said. "We live hand to mouth. Half the time I can't even afford to fix my car and put it in shape to win, because I have to give all my money to your mama for food."

Dale was stunned into silence. He hadn't realized just how bad things were.

"You see how I lay back in every race and wait for the last few laps to make my charge? You know why I do that? I wait because I can't afford to take a chance on wrecking. If I ever wrecked this car, I couldn't afford another one. I'd have to go back to the mill, at my age. Now tell me—you wanna live like that?"

"I won't have to," Dale replied.

"Is that so?"

"I'll make enough money to get by."

Ralph raised one eyebrow. "Oh, yeah? How you gonna do that? Racing?" He let out a short laugh. "You ain't even old enough to be a driver till next year. Anyway, you'll never make it as a driver—you ain't tough enough."

Dale blinked back tears. No way was he going to let his father see him cry. Not now. Not after what he'd just said.

"Maybe tough enough to be a good mechanic, but that's all," Ralph went on. "And don't think I'm gonna start payin' you to help me here either."

"I . . . I can get a job as a mechanic at some shop in town. They'll hire me if you recommend me. That way, I can save up enough to race cars in a year or so."

Ralph considered this. "You ain't even that good a mechanic yet," he said. "Good for sixteen, but there's grown men out there that need those kinds of jobs to feed their families. No shop owner's going to turn them away and give the job to some sixteen-year-old kid."

Dale was silent. He didn't know what to say.

Ralph took a rag from his pocket and wiped the grease off his hands. "Now you go back to school tomorrow and tell them you made a mistake leaving. I'm going on into the house. You can put those axle keys in yourself, if you're such a hotshot mechanic."

He threw the rag in the trash bin. "Leaving school was the worst mistake I ever made in my life," he said. "I'll be jiggered if I let my son do the same dumb thing."

He opened the shop door and slammed it shut behind him, leaving Dale standing there holding the number six.

He got to work putting the new part in.

But he wasn't going to go back to school tomorrow, no matter what his daddy said.

He wasn't going back to school ever again.

Work and Family
1969–1971

No matter what his parents said or did, Dale refused to go back to school. Not even the offer of a brand-new car was enough to make him return to the classroom.

His dad held it against him for a year and a half. He let Dale keep working with him in the shop, but he barely said two words to him.

Worse, there was tension in the air between the two of them. It made Dale want to go out on his own and get away from the house.

That was what led him into Letanye's

arms. By the time Dale was eighteen, the two of them were married with a baby on the way.

Dale knew it took a lot of money to support a family once there were children, so he took any job he could find—anything to help him put away some money. He worked at several different garages—welding, aligning front ends, fixing brakes, and every other job you could do on a car.

These jobs helped him understand all the little things that affected a car's performance. He stored it all away in his head for the future.

He had set himself the goal of racing a car one year after quitting school. In the end, it took him a little longer. He was nineteen before he finally made it out onto the short dirt tracks of North Carolina, doing what he'd waited all his life to do.

The car was Letanye's brother's—a six-cylinder 1956 Ford Club Sedan. It looked like a family car, not a real race car.

Dale and his friends decided a paint job would help it look scarier. They tried to paint it avocado, which would go with the purple roof—but they mixed the paint wrong, and it came out pink!

That was the car Dale Earnhardt drove in his first race, at Concord Speedway. Pink, with a purple roof—not exactly intimidating! DAYVAULT'S TUNE-UP & BRAKE SERVICE was painted in black on the fenders, and K-2 and DALE on the doors.

He was a natural from the very start. David Oliver, who also drove that night, said, "You could tell that he knew what he was doing. All those years with Ralph—he wasn't like someone starting out. . . . He knew when to make the move and when not to make the move. He knew where the holes were."

Dale didn't win that first race, but he did something much more important. He proved to himself—and to everyone else who was there that night—that he belonged in a race car.

After the race he had to get himself another car, because his brother-in-law wanted to race the pink one himself.

But where to get one?

Dale turned to his daddy for help. After a year and a half of chilly relations, Ralph had finally accepted Dale's decision to leave school.

He sent Dale over to James Miller's house. Miller was a race car driver who'd lost both his legs in a racetrack accident the year before. He had a couple of Ford Falcons sitting in a junkyard he kept behind his house.

Dale asked if he could race one of them, and Miller said yes—if Dale would do some work fixing it up.

Dale went to it right there and then. He worked all night, then went straight to his welding job at the Great Dane Trucking Company.

The next night he was back at Miller's again to continue working on his new ride. From that day forward, he spent less and less time at home with Letanye and little Kerry. For the next year he raced that car as much as he could.

More than half the time, though, it was in the shop, because Dale was constantly bashing it up. It had to do with the way he drove. He would bang into other drivers to force them into the wall or onto the grass, ramming them from behind to create a hole where there was none.

"He was just trying things, seeing what he could do," Miller remembers. "He'd see a hole and think he could make it through. Sometimes he could, sometimes he couldn't. Ralph would talk to him, teach him what to do."

The following year, Miller and Dale built a new car—at Ralph's garage, and with Ralph's help. It was another '56 Falcon, but this one was put together better, and Dale didn't crash it as much.

That year he won the first race of his life—at Concord Speedway. He won a few more races that year too.

When James Miller sold his car to the Russell Brothers in Concord, North Carolina, Dale went with it. He had a wife and baby back at home, but he couldn't think about that—he was off and running.

After a third-place finish one night, he brought the one hundred dollars in prize money home to show his mom. Martha smiled, but she didn't take it from him. "I'm happy for you, Dale," she said. "You keep the money. You and Letanye need it for the baby."

"It's rent, Mama," Dale told her. "For the trailer."

Ever since the wedding, the young couple had lived in a small camper that sat in the driveway of his parents' house.

"Well, if it's the rent, then you'd best give it to your daddy yourself," Martha said, giving him back the money.

He went out back to the shop, where Ralph was busy doing some welding. Dale held out the money to him. "Look, Daddy," he said, venturing a smile. "I won tonight."

Ralph stared deep into his eyes, not smiling. "How much is it?"

"A hundred dollars. Take it—it's for the back rent."

Ralph took the money and stuffed it into his pocket. "A hundred dollars is chicken feed, boy."

"Well, there'll be more where that came from," Dale told him.

"Maybe so," Ralph said. "But how much more? You'll never make any real money racing on dirt. You'll only end up like me—working in the mill or in someone's garage."

It made him furious that his dad was so tough on him.

Well, Dale would show him. No matter what it took, he was going to keep on racing cars.

If his daddy could hang on into his forties as a driver, why then, so could Dale! He was twenty years younger, and he knew deep down in his bones how to drive a race car.

One day he'd be as good as Ironheart—even better! He might have a lot to learn yet, but he would learn it. He had more than talent and courage—he had a fierce determination. It burned like a roaring fire inside him.

Nobody was going to tell Dale Earnhardt what he could or couldn't achieve—not even his daddy.

"The problem is, my cars aren't fast enough," he told Letanye as she bounced baby Kerry on her knees. "It takes money to buy better parts, and I've got to finish in the top three to make that extra money."

"Maybe if you just raced once in a while—" she began, but he cut her off.

"How'm I supposed to become the greatest

racer in the world if I don't do it every chance I get?"

"Maybe you should race more carefully, like your daddy," she said. "Here, you wanna hold him for a while?"

She handed Kerry over, and he hoisted the baby up, looking into his eyes. "What do you think, Kerry?" he asked his little son. "You think I should do like your grandpa? He lays back in the weeds till the last few laps, so he doesn't wreck his car. Then he sprints to the front all at once, like this!"

Making an engine noise, Dale ran around the little room, bouncing the baby as he went. Little Kerry's eyes went wide, but he seemed to enjoy the ride.

"Cut it out, Dale," said Letanye. "You'll make him spit up."

Dale sat down and handed the baby back to her. "I can't race like my daddy," he told her. "We're different people. He's low-key, and I'm . . ."

"Reckless?" she finished for him.

"Reckless? You think I'm reckless?"

"How many times have you wrecked already, Dale? How do you expect to buy better parts for your car if you have to spend all your money on repairs?"

"I'm not my daddy," he said again. "And I can't drive like him. I can only drive like *me*—goin' hell bent for leather from the minute the green flag comes down."

Maybe it was just stubbornness, but Dale kept on doing things his way, both on and off the track. The month before he'd quarreled with his boss at the garage and gotten himself fired. Next thing he knew—to his own shock and surprise—he was working shifts at the fabric mill.

"Just another lint head," his dad had said.

But what choice did he have? Letanye and little Kerry had to eat, didn't they?

Even with Dale's regular paycheck, they were still falling behind in their rent. They'd had to get their own place that year—the trailer was just too small for the three of them.

One night soon after that, he came home from a race after finishing fourth—just out of the money.

The minute he walked through the door, he knew something was different. The whole place was ice cold.

"Did I forget to buy propane for the tank or something?" he asked his wife.

"Forget? Dale, what were you going to pay for it with?"

"I get paid on Friday at the mill," he said. "We can make it till then."

"Are you kidding me?" she shouted, her breath coming out as smoke in the chilly air. "Our baby will have frozen to death by then!"

"Well, I don't know what else to tell you, Letanye. There hasn't been much money comin' in from racing, but my luck's bound to change soon. I'm getting to be a better driver every week."

"You haven't won in six months, Dale," she reminded him. "Look, why don't you just swallow your pride and ask your daddy for a loan?"

"How many times have you asked me that? A thousand?" he shot back. "I've told you, he doesn't have that much to give. My parents have got four other kids at home, remember?"

"Well, I can't take this any more, that's all I know," she said, her expression hardening. "And neither can the baby."

"Listen, honey, I'll tell you what. I'm gonna quit the mill and start racing full-time. I can't take being a lint head, anyway—and if I really put all my time into racing, I know I can start winning again."

She stared at him as if he were from Mars. "Have you even heard a word I've said?" she asked him.

"Sure, darlin'," he said. "I know it's hard, but we'll make it through."

"Will you ask your daddy for a loan or not?" she said, her chin starting to tremble.

"I . . . I just can't."

She started to cry then, and that made the baby wail.

"Come on now, Letanye," he said, trying to give her a hug.

She yanked her shoulder away from his hand. "Take me to my mother's," she demanded.

"Right now?"

"Right now. I'm not gonna let our baby freeze to death."

"Sure, honey. But . . . but you'll come back as soon as I've got the heat going again. Won't you?"

She said nothing. She just stood there, staring at the floor.

"Won't you?" he repeated.

But she still wouldn't say a word.

Two Families
1972–1973

Dale and Letanye were divorced now. She had a new husband, Jack, a nice guy who made a good living and didn't race cars.

Dale missed Letanye, but he could see she was happier this way. It was better for her and for the baby, too.

So when she came to Dale one day and said that Jack wanted to adopt Kerry and become his legal father, Dale said yes.

It wasn't an easy decision for him—he loved that baby deep, deep in his heart—but he knew he couldn't be a proper father to him. Not now, when he had no money and no sure prospects for the future.

Jack would love Kerry and take good care of him. He'd be a real father to the boy.

Dale waved good-bye as the three of them took off in their car. He had to bite his lip to stop the tears from coming as his little boy waved good-bye to him. Dale wondered if he'd ever see Kerry again.

Martha Earnhardt came out the door—Dale was living at home again, till he got back on his feet. "What's going on, Dale?" she asked.

When he told her, she broke down. He explained how it was better this way, but it was no use. Martha had just lost her grandchild, and she couldn't stop crying.

Finally he gave up and went back to the shop, where his father was working on the latest version of car number 8.

"Why's your mama so upset?" he asked Dale.

"I'm letting Jack adopt Kerry," Dale told

him. "I can't provide for a baby. Not yet. Not till I make it as a driver."

Ralph stood there, nodding, taking the news in slowly. Then he shook his head in disgust. "Boy, when are you gonna learn what it takes to be a man?"

"I know what it takes, Daddy," Dale said. "It takes what neither one of us has got—money. But I'll have money one day soon. You'll see. I'm a good driver, and I'm getting better all the time."

"Is that right?" Ralph asked. "You think so, do you?"

"I'll prove it to you, Daddy," Dale said, his jaw tight. "Next week at Metrolina Speedway. I'll be racing there. You come too, and I'll prove to you what kind of driver I am."

Ralph Earnhardt showed up to race, all right—but he and Dale were in different divisions: Dale in the semi-Modified, Ralph in the Sportsman.

But that night, not enough Sportsman racers had shown up, so the owner of the track announced that the top five finishers in the semi-Modified would be allowed to race in the Sportsman race.

Dale finished first in his race and let out a yell of triumph. He and his daddy were going to go head-to-head for the first time!

Ralph's car was much faster than Dale's, of course. In fact, it was the fastest car there that night. By the time the race was nearly over, Ralph had almost lapped the entire field.

Dale was running in fourth place, right behind the guy who'd almost beaten him in the earlier race. The other driver's car was stronger, and no matter how hard he tried, Dale hadn't been able to pass him. He desperately wanted to finish in the money, just to show his daddy what a good driver he was getting to be.

Then, looking in his rearview mirror, Dale

saw number 8 come up on his back bumper. Dale swerved to the inside to let his father go by. But instead of sweeping past Dale, Ralph just swerved right along with him.

Twice more Dale tried to get out of his father's way with the same result.

Before he could figure out what was going on, he felt his dad's car bump into his. The impact made Dale's car shoot forward. Again, number 8 banged into Dale's rear end. And again. And again—until Dale was dead even with the third place car. There was one more heavy impact, and Dale passed his rival.

Now Ralph's car shot by them, heading for the checkered flag. For one last lap, Dale managed to stay ahead of the car he'd just passed. He ended up finishing third—in the money, thanks to his dad!

Dale was glad to have earned a little cash, but most of all he felt embarrassed. He knew he wouldn't have come out with a dime that night if it hadn't been for his father. His dad had shown him up, made him look bad—humiliated him, in fact.

The other drivers in pit row were all sneering at him, shaking their heads. They all knew what had happened, and they didn't like it one bit. "Daddy's boy," they whispered, mocking him.

Dale looked over at victory lane, where his father was holding up the trophy. Ralph saw him and gave him a meaningful look, as if to say, "You're not the great driver you think you are, boy. Not yet, anyway."

Dale stormed off the track, his insides churning. It had been exciting, racing with his dad for the first time. But Ralph Earnhardt had given him a lesson he wouldn't soon forget.

Especially since the two would never run in the same race again.

Someone was waving to him from over by one of the trailers. Brenda—his new girlfriend. She was crazy about Dale, and he about her. He went over and hugged her, lifting her up off the ground and spinning her around while she laughed and kissed him.

"One hundred bucks!" he said, showing her the cash he'd won. "Come on, baby, let's go have ourselves a good time!"

Soon, they were married. And pretty soon after that, they had a baby daughter, Kelley.

It was a good thing Letanye had married Jack, Dale thought. If she hadn't, he would have had to send her money every month for Kerry.

He missed his son, but Dale was glad the boy was provided for. As it was, Dale had all he could do to support his new wife and baby.

He kept on racing, although he had to hold down jobs in garages so he could keep his cars running. He was a reckless racer, always banging other cars out of the way.

It made him a dangerous man, not just for

71

the other drivers, but also for himself. And every time he wrecked his car, he had to start all over again. Sometimes he had to hold down two jobs at once just to keep up.

Whenever he wasn't working, he was racing. In fact, he was gone so often that he hardly ever had time for Brenda and the baby.

"You have two families, Dale," she said to him over and over again. "Us, and racing."

He knew it was true, but he just couldn't help himself. "All I want to do is race," he explained to her. "I know I can do this, baby. Deep inside, I know I've got what it takes."

He was a talented driver—there was no doubt in his mind about that. Talented enough to go all the way to the top.

He'd even earned a nickname for himself— one modeled after his father's. The other drivers had started calling Dale "Iron*head*."

The name was supposed to be an insult, making him out to be stupid and a little bit crazy. But Dale kind of liked it.

If being Ironhead meant he was willing to drive those other cars into the wall, well then, it was a good name for him.

That year, 1973, he'd won seventeen races in the Russell Brothers' car. Seventeen! He'd taken home a whopping $3,600 in prize money. To Dale, it was a fortune. But his daddy just laughed when Dale told him how much he'd won. As far as he was concerned, $3,600 was nothing.

And Brenda wasn't impressed either. It might have seemed like a lot of money to Dale, but she knew better. She was from a racing family herself.

Even when he won an incredible thirty-six races the following year, there was still never enough money—Dale had to keep pouring every dollar into fixing his car every time he wrecked it.

Aside from his winnings on the track, he was making a little over a hundred dollars a week working at Punchy's Wheel Alignment

in Concord. He was working there on the night of September 26, 1973, when a woman came into the shop to tell him that his father was sick and had been taken to the hospital.

But the news was even worse than that— the woman hadn't had the heart to tell Dale that his daddy was dead.

Ralph Earnhardt had suffered a fatal heart attack in his shop at the age of forty-five.

Dale Earnhardt had lost his daddy.

The Trip to Rock Bottom
1973–1977

They buried Ralph Earnhardt in the Center Grove Lutheran Cemetery in Kannapolis. They ordered him a headstone in the shape of a race car with a number 8 carved on the side.

Dale sold off his daddy's two hunting dogs. He couldn't bear to be with them any more—they reminded him too much of all those good times in the woods with his daddy, stalking game and fishing.

It was a bleak Christmas that year. His mother had taken her husband's death even harder than Dale. Money was tight, and now without the family's major breadwinner around, it would get even tighter.

Dale, now twenty-two years old, was learning his craft, becoming a better driver with every passing year. But that didn't mean he was making any more money.

He was still wrecking cars left and right. Even when he didn't, the wear and tear from the way he drove meant lots of repairs—in other words, nearly every dollar he made got poured right into his racing.

He tried riding on asphalt since the prize money was better. But soon he had to give it up because he wrecked too many cars at those higher speeds, and he had no money left to keep going.

Dirt track purses were smaller, and so he brought home less money. Their family car was a two-hundred-dollar hunk of junk, because they couldn't afford anything better.

He and Brenda wound up living in a double-wide trailer in the driveway of the house on Sedan Avenue. Dale fixed up his daddy's garage and reopened it, with a canopy added so he could work outside when the weather was right. He worked on other people's cars, doing tune-ups and repairs, in between working on his own car for the next race.

Dale took out short-term loans so he could keep racing. He just knew that if he could keep at it long enough, he could turn his career—and his life—around.

When he needed to relax, to get away from it all, he went hunting or fishing. He'd done that with his daddy since he was a little kid, and it was still his favorite way to unwind. Of course, he didn't take Brenda along. She had to stay home and watch their daughter.

Things were going from bad to worse, but Dale refused to quit. The only solution, he decided, was to somehow get enough money to put together a car that could really compete on the asphalt tracks of the Sportsman Division, with its higher prize money.

So in 1974 he took out some more loans, bought a used car that looked promising, and broke the news to Brenda, who was pregnant with their son, Dale Jr., at the time.

She was not happy, but with a new baby on the way, she wasn't in any condition to move out. In any case, Dale convinced her to stick around long enough to give him a real chance at breaking through.

The Sportsman Division of NASCAR had grown in the past few years. It was now something like AAA in baseball—the highest of the minor leagues. Drivers could make a decent living on the circuit if they were good, and if they were careful.

Cars and costs on the Sportsman Circuit were almost as expensive as the Winston Cup Circuit—racing's major league. So most drivers steered clear of crashes. It was different from the dirt tracks in that way.

But Dale was a dirt track driver at heart. He drove on the asphalt, at those higher speeds, with the same crazy abandon he displayed on the dirt ovals. In fact, he was even wilder and more reckless on the asphalt than ever before.

Maybe it was the fact that his daddy wasn't around anymore, looking over his shoulder. Ralph had been like an extra set of brakes for Dale. Now those brakes were gone.

Ralph had never hurt himself badly in a race car—a broken foot was the worst he'd suffered. Dale raced like he didn't care what happened to him. He went for the front of the pack from the moment the green flag came down. He'd nudge you or slam into you or run you into a wall if he had to—and he never let up till the race was over or his car was done.

The other drivers would get mad at him, naturally. Some of them downright hated Ironhead.

But Dale didn't care. He understood how they felt. He'd try to be friendly in response, saying, "Don't hold it against me. Don't be mad. You do the same to me next week." And he'd give them that trademark crooked smile.

Some forgave him. Some didn't.

He was racing most days of the week now, trying to break through to where he could make a real living at it. He was borrowing and borrowing, putting himself and his family in a deeper and deeper hole. And he was almost never home.

Even when he was home, he was usually out at the local garages, hunting for a better, faster ride. Anything to get an edge on the track.

One garage he stopped in was Tommy Houston's. Tommy had been a driver himself—a pretty good one too. Tommy's niece happened to be there that day—a pretty sixteen-year-old named Teresa. Dale was shocked when Tommy

81

told him Teresa was going to college that September. She'd finished all her high school courses a year early, so they'd let her graduate.

Pretty and smart, too.

He didn't think much about the encounter, but Teresa Houston remembered it. It would turn out to be a key moment in Dale Earnhardt's life—he just didn't know it yet.

Another garage Dale visited soon after, still looking to upgrade his car, was Ed Negre's. Ed was a driver and a car owner, too. He'd just finished building a new one and was showing it off to Dale, while his son Norman hung out in the garage with them.

"That's a beauty," Dale said, admiring it.

"Yup," Negre replied. "I'm racing her in the Charlotte 600 next month."

Dale wished he could be the one behind the wheel, but he knew that wouldn't happen. The Charlotte 600 was part of the Winston Cup Circuit. Dale had never even driven in a Winston Cup race.

"What are you doin' with your other car—the old one?" Dale asked, thinking he might buy the big, heavy Dodge if he could scrounge up a few more loans. There had to be two or three of his friends he hadn't asked for money yet. . . .

"Say, Dad," Norman Negre suddenly said. "What about entering both cars at the 600 and lettin' Dale here drive the old one?"

Ed Negre raised an eyebrow. "Son, I know you want to be a crew chief, but—"

"You're right, Dad. I do want to be a crew chief—and this is the perfect chance for me to try! Dale's a great driver."

"That may be, but you boys'll never get her qualified for that race. The car's just not fast enough for Winston Cup."

"Give us a chance, Dad," Norman pleaded.

Ed Negre still wasn't sold, though. Not until Norman brought him to a Sportsman's race that Dale was competing in the next weekend at Metrolina Speedway.

Dale zoomed to the front of the pack right away, but Ed Negre remained unconvinced. There were lots of good young racers. He didn't see anything special about this kid Earnhardt.

Then, in mid-race, Dale blew a tire and had to pull into the pit. He lost the lead and Negre's interest, too.

The car owner was watching the other drivers a few minutes later, when he was startled to see Earnhardt racing back toward the front of the pack. "How'd he do that?" he asked aloud. "He was way back there. . . ."

A few laps later Dale had to return to the pit again for an engine problem. This time he lost even more time. But once again he drove himself back into the race. Yet another time, he had to pit, but incredibly, he kept on gaining ground until he was back in the lead!

"You know what, son?" Ed Negre said to Norman. "This guy can drive."

So the deal was done. Dale wanted to shout it out to the whole world—after all he'd suffered and sacrificed, he was finally getting his big break!

Or was he?

Winston Cup was only four years old in 1975. It had a thirty-one-race yearly circuit, with points kept for how well you did in each race. The winner of the cup was the team with the most points at the end of the year.

It was a different way of thinking and a different way of driving. Since winning each individual race mattered less than total points for the year, there was even less bumping and grinding in Winston Cup than in the Sportsman Division.

There was another difference too. Winston Cup was dominated by three or four teams, each sponsored by the big car companies. The Wood Brothers, the Pettys, and Junior Johnson won just about every race. All the other drivers just jockeyed for points, happy to take home the earnings for placing well down in the pack.

But that was not the way Dale Earnhardt drove. It wasn't the way he thought. And he wasn't about to change himself now, just to make the most of his big break.

When his friend Humpy Wheeler warned him before the race to take it easy on the car since it was bought with Negre's mortgage, Dale replied, "I can't win if I'm worried about wreckin'."

It was a six-hundred-mile race. Dale had never even gone half that long, and he had no idea what to expect. Negre warned him to take extra water along, but Dale laughed him off—only to have to go to the pit once during the race just for a drink!

It took Dale awhile to get used to driving such a fast, well-made, expensive car. It was so hard to control! When he went into the corners, it felt like he was holding the world by the steering wheel. Soon, though, he got the hang of it—in fact, he loved it!

He and Norman got the car qualified all

right—in thirty-third position. Dale started the race way back there, but he finished twenty-second—two places ahead of Negre, in his newer, faster, better car.

Richard Petty, the greatest driver in the history of the sport at that time—nicknamed "The King"—lapped Dale five times on his way to victory. But Dale didn't care—he was thrilled! He'd run a great race in a car that was strictly second-rate by Winston Cup standards.

It might have been second-rate, but it was still the fastest, best car he'd ever driven. He was eager for more—and he was sure it would happen too.

But it didn't. Negre couldn't afford to keep two cars going at the same time.

He tried to work something out with another owner, but the man refused, saying of Dale Earnhardt, "He ain't nobody."

"Oh yes, he is," Negre replied. "He's going to be a superstar."

He was right, but it still would be many

years before the world woke up to a driver by the name of Dale Earnhardt.

In 1976, at the age of twenty-five, Dale got another chance at Winston Cup racing. It was in the Dixie 500 at Atlanta, subbing for Johnny Ray, who'd hurt himself at Daytona and couldn't drive. Ray watched from the sidelines as Dale took his car and went for broke with it.

He was running a good race when, near the end, the driver ahead of him lost his steering. Dale plowed right into him, and his car went airborne. It flipped over several times in the worst accident in the seventeen-year history of the track.

Everyone thought Dale must be dead. There was no way anyone could survive a wreck like that—was there?

Then Dale emerged from the car and waved to the crowd. Incredibly, all he had was a cut on his hand!

He had been lucky to escape with his life. The car, however, was ruined, and Johnny Ray couldn't afford another one. He was out of business, and Dale, whom he otherwise would have hired as his regular driver, was out of a job again.

Dale was frustrated beyond belief. He'd been doing so well, and the crash had been no fault of his own! Yet he was somehow being punished for it. There was no choice but to go back to dirt track racing, driving for his father-in-law, Robert Gee.

His wife had had enough. Brenda left him, taking the children with her. For the second time in his life, Dale had failed to hold his family together. He was alone again.

It was one of the worst times of his life. Luckily, he'd made a new friend—a race car driver from Alabama by the name of Neil Bonnett.

The two had met during a race on the

Sportsman Circuit. During the race, Dale had bumped into a lot of the other cars on his way to victory lane. Bonnett had been one of those drivers, but he'd come out okay.

Dick Sinder, however, had wrecked, and he wanted revenge.

After the race Humpy Wheeler was congratulating Dale. He was telling Dale how much of his father's talent he had when Sinder came running up the gangway waving a pistol and shouting Dale's name.

Dale took off running, jumped the fence, and picked his way through the woods to the main road, where he was picked up by a truck—driven by none other than Neil Bonnett.

The two men hit it off right away. Each was tougher than nails on the outside, tender on the inside. Both of them had the same dry sense of humor. And both of them loved hunting, fishing, and, of course, racing cars.

During the loneliest time of Dale's life, it

was Bonnett who took him out hunting and fishing. It was Bonnett in whom Dale confided his hopes, his dreams, and his fears. They weren't that far apart in years, but for Dale, it was like having an older brother.

"All I want is to be a regular on the Winston Cup Circuit," Dale said on a fishing trip they took in 1978. They sat in a rowboat out in the middle of a woodland lake, casting for bass, as the sun set over the hills to the west. "I feel like I'm really ready to compete at that level too. But people keep tellin' me I should quit drivin'."

"Which people?"

"Brenda . . . a lot of my friends. They all think I'm crazy."

"Well, what do you think?" Bonnett asked.

Dale shrugged. "Maybe they're right," he said. "I mean, I'm twenty-seven years old, Neil. My daddy was dead by the time he was forty-five. How many years do I even have left?"

"Lots of drivers don't make it till they're your age," Bonnett said.

"Oh, yeah? Name one."

Bonnett couldn't think of any. Most of the successful NASCAR drivers had established themselves by the age of twenty-four or twenty-five. "You're doin' better and better," he told Dale. "How many times have you driven Winston Cup this year?"

"Five," Dale said. He yanked on his line, thinking he had a fish, but it was only a lily pad. Dale reeled in, disgusted. "I've had seven races in Winston Cup over the past two years, but they were all just strokin'. None of those cars ever had a chance to win. Their owners didn't have the money to compete with the big boys."

He turned to his friend and looked him straight in the eye. "Maybe that's all I'll ever be, a stroker."

"Aw, come on, Dale, don't talk like that."

"I mean, if I do give it up, I can always

race on Saturday nights at the old Concord Speedway, just to race. That's what I care about the most, after all. . . . Yeah, maybe I should just get a job and quit worrying about making money at racing. I mean, I've been borrowin' money from everyone I know. I can't keep that up much longer. . . ."

Bonnett sat still, letting the quiet of the lake settle on both of them. He said nothing, feeling that Dale had more to get off his chest.

"On the other hand, I've been doin' better since Brenda left and took the kids. It sounds strange, doesn't it? But it's true—I've won seventeen dirt track races this year alone. I know I'm getting better all the time. And I was talkin' the other day with Bobby Isaac— he was a friend of my dad's. He watched me grow up, and he's seen me drive lots of times. He said I ought to stop workin' on cars, and start concentrate on drivin' if I want to succeed."

94

"Mmmm. So?"

"Well, I was wonderin' . . . what do *you* think?"

"Me? Well, I think you're a talented driver, Dale. I think you're just one break away from bein' a star in this business." He winked. "But then, what do I know?"

Encouraged by Bobby Isaac and Neil Bonnett, Dale decided he could hang on just a little while longer.

It was a good thing he did. If he'd quit then, in early 1978, he would never have gone on to be the face of NASCAR—and perhaps the greatest driver who ever lived.

The Big Breakthrough
1978

Dale's kids were growing up—the youngest, Dale Jr., was almost four years old now. Both he and Kelley would tell their dad, when they spoke to him on the phone or saw him every other weekend, that they wanted to be race car drivers too—just like him. They were living with Brenda, the three of them in a little rented house.

Dale never heard from his older son, Kerry, but he thought of him often and wondered how he was doing. He was sure he'd made the right move, letting Jack adopt Kerry. Dale knew he wouldn't have been as good a dad to him, what with having no money and always being off somewhere racing. But that didn't mean he didn't miss him.

Like Dale's children, the sport of auto racing was growing. Its governing body, NASCAR, which had been born in 1949 (just two years before Dale's birth), had gotten stronger and more popular. New asphalt super-speedways were being built all over the southeastern United States, and even some across the country.

The Winston Cup series especially was booming. This was mainly because the "Big Three" auto companies—General Motors, Ford, and Chrysler—had stopped sponsoring teams directly. Instead, they made their top-of-the-line racing equipment—the pride of their research and development departments— available to everyone.

This meant that instead of three or four teams dominating the points standings every season, anyone willing to invest enough money could put together a team that could win a championship.

At first not many owners jumped at the opportunity. Outside the southeast, racing hadn't caught on quite as much. But one businessman who did jump in with both feet was Rod Osterlund of California. He looked NASCAR over and decided to put together a winning Winston Cup team.

Osterlund was decidedly not a stroker. From the very beginning, he had his sights set on winning a championship. He bought the best equipment he could find and got together a top team of mechanics. He hired a team leader, Roland Wlodyka, and a driver, Dave Marcis, for the 1978 season.

He gave all his workers bonuses for doing well and lots of fringe benefits like health insurance—something new for a NASCAR team.

All of this raised a few eyebrows among

the other Winston Cup teams. Who was this Osterlund fellow, anyway—this outsider from California who thought he could teach all the old Southern boys how to run their business?

Lots of them were curious. And one of the people who frequently wandered into the Osterlund shop to take a peek at what they were up to, and maybe buy a few used parts, was Dale Earnhardt.

The Osterlund car was one of the best in the 1978 field. But its owner and crew chief were not happy with their driver. Dave Marcis was too careful. He didn't wreck the car, but he never really took any big chances either. He finished third, fourth, or fifth plenty of times, but he never won a race for them. Careful, respectable, competent, surely. But not the brilliant driver they needed to make their team a Winston Cup champion.

Toward the end of the 1978 season Osterlund and Wlodyka decided to run a second car in the last race of the season along with the one Dave Marcis was driving.

The idea was not a new one, but it hadn't been done very often. The idea was that one driver could help the other by running interference for him, blocking the other cars, creating a good draft, and opening holes for the faster car to dash through.

Osterlund wanted to try it before the season ended. He targeted the Dixie 500 in Atlanta. If the tactic worked, he figured, they could run two cars for the entire 1979 season.

For his second car, Osterlund didn't have enough money to start from scratch with all new parts. So he bought a Chevy Monte Carlo that had been wrecked by Benny Parsons, had his mechanics fix it up, and painted the number 98 on it. He bought a trailer that could carry the two cars to the race at the same time.

Now all he needed was a driver for his second car.

Wlodyka recommended Dale Earnhardt, but Osterlund wasn't convinced.

Humpy Wheeler, who had become well-known around the NASCAR world, had known Dale for years, and his father before him. He also put in a good word for Earnhardt. "It's been a long time since I've seen a youngster so determined, so hungry," he said. "If nothing happens to sour his attitude, I think he's going to be a star in a few years—and a big one."

"It's not just determination, Humpy," Osterlund said. "It takes talent, too."

"Oh, he's got that," Wheeler insisted. "Great drivers can see things other drivers can't—and Dale's got those kind of eyes."

Osterlund still hesitated. "I don't know. . . ."

"He's a local guy too," Wheeler said. "The fans like that. And I'll tell you what—just to sweeten the deal for you, I'll give you five thousand dollars to put Dale behind the wheel of that car."

"Five thousand? That's a lot of money, Humpy."

"I know it. But you ought to watch him race once. You'll see why I'm willing to put my money where my mouth is."

Wheeler brought Osterlund to meet Dale before a Sportsman Circuit race. Dale didn't exactly make a great impression. He was twice divorced and nearly bankrupt, with wild hair and torn jeans. In the race, he drove "like a maniac," according to Osterlund.

Still, with Wheeler's money as a convincer, Osterlund agreed to give Dale a chance. More of an audition, really, on the Sportsman Circuit. He had a car thrown together out of spare parts and let Dale drive it at Charlotte in October.

Dale came in second in that race—a truly impressive performance in a less-than-perfect car. Osterlund and Wheeler shook on the deal, and Dale got his big chance—his *last* big chance. He had already decided—if this race didn't lead to a career in Winston Cup, he was going to hang it up and finally quit trying to race cars for a living.

For the race in Atlanta—the last race of that year's Winston Cup series—Dale drove Osterlund's second car, while Marcis drove his number one ride.

Still, by racing like a maniac, bumping drivers out of the way left and right, Dale managed to pass more than twenty cars and come in fourth—just one spot behind Dave Marcis.

It was an incredible performance considering Dale had been driving a strictly second-rate car. Osterlund was duly impressed.

Dale had just finished the race and was in the parking lot, picking up his kids for the weekend. Brenda shook her head as he gave Kelley and Dale Jr. big hugs. "You're behind on the child support again, Dale," she reminded him.

"I know it," he said. "I'll get you the money by next week."

"Sure you will," she said. "Dale, when are you gonna quit this craziness?"

"You mean driving?"

"You know that's what I mean."

"Look, Brenda, I'll get you the money for the kids, okay? You think I like being a deadbeat dad? I'm trying to win some races here so I can get the money for them. Cut me some slack, okay?"

She just shook her head and sighed. "Have them back to me by eight o'clock tomorrow night." With that, she walked off toward her car, leaving Dale with his children.

Just then, some racing fans came up to him and asked for autographs. When he'd finished signing, he reached down and took Kelley's hand. Then he reached for Dale Jr.'s—but the boy had disappeared!

"Dale!" he called out. "Dale Jr.!"

He looked around the parking lot, but there was no sign of the boy. Pulling Kelley behind him, he walked back toward the track, passing through knots of people still buzzing about the excitement of the race.

There was the race's winner, Darrell Waltrip, talking to reporters. "That guy Earnhardt's just plain nuts," he was saying, "bumping into everybody like that." He caught sight of Dale and frowned. "Crazy," he repeated, spitting on the ground in disgust.

Dale ignored him. He was worried about finding his son, and besides, he never cared what other drivers thought of him. He figured if they liked him, he wasn't being aggressive enough on the track.

Still, many of the Sportsman Circuit drivers were friendly with him, because they knew that when he was off the track, Dale was just a regular guy like the rest of them.

Dale spotted Dale Jr. over in a corner, crying. A pretty girl with lush dark hair and sparkling eyes was squatting down next to him. She was dabbing the boy's eyes with a tissue and trying to comfort him.

When he saw his father, Dale Jr. yelled "Daddy!" and rushed over to him, leaping up into Dale's arms.

The pretty girl walked over to them. "Howdy," she said, offering Dale her hand and smiling. "He seems a lot happier now."

"Thank you for minding him," Dale said. "I, uh . . . I don't know how he took off so fast like that."

"He's fast like his daddy," the girl said, flashing a brilliant smile. "Nice to see you again, Dale."

He blinked. The girl looked familiar, now that he thought about it. "You're . . . Tommy Houston's niece, right? Goin' off to college?"

"That's right," she said. "Teresa."

"Teresa! Sure, I remember you."

"I remember you too." She looked into his eyes, then down at the kids.

"Oh, excuse me," Dale said. "This is Kelley, and you already know Junior."

Teresa shook hands with Kelly and patted

Dale Jr. on the head. Then she looked around. "Where's your wife?" she asked.

"Oh, she took off," he answered. "I mean, I've got the kids for the weekend."

"Oh. I see."

Dale cleared his throat. "You, ah . . . you wanna go get some lunch?"

She smiled and scrunched up her shoulders. "I thought you'd never ask," she said.

They were eating lunch when a man in a cowboy hat entered the restaurant, followed by four or five other men.

"That's Richard Petty," he told Teresa. "The King."

"I know who he is," she said.

"The greatest racer of all time," Dale said. "He's won a bunch of Winston Cup Championships—way more than anybody else."

Teresa gave him a long look. "You're a great racer too," she said.

"Aw, no," Dale said, embarrassed. "I can't compare to that guy."

"Not yet. But someday," she insisted.

"Oh, come on," he said.

"Why not?" she asked. "I saw how you raced today. Nobody can thread a needle between two cars like you can. Nobody has the feel for the track and the car that you have."

Dale was impressed with her manner, her confidence. Teresa was smart as well as pretty—and she sure got along well with his kids.

Even better, she liked the fact that he raced cars! He'd never been around a woman who liked that about him before.

"I was actually thinking of quitting," he told her.

"You were not."

"I was."

"But you've made it to Winston Cup!" she said.

"I'm still broke," he said with a shrug.

"Besides, I've gotten to Winston Cup seven times before. None of them ever led to anything."

"You're gonna make it," she told him, looking him right in the eye.

"How do you know?"

She shrugged. "I just do."

The door of the restaurant opened, and Rod Osterlund walked in. He looked around until he saw Dale, then walked over to their table.

"Earnhardt!" he said, reaching out his hand. "That was some good driving out there today."

"Thanks, Mr. Osterlund," Dale said. Then he introduced him to Teresa.

"Listen," Osterlund said, "I've got to ask you something, Earnhardt. Can we talk?"

Dale looked at Teresa, then back at Osterlund. "Sure," he said. "What's on your mind, sir?"

"Dave Marcis just quit on me."

110

Dale sat up straight, alert and excited.

"I need a driver for next season, and I'm considering asking you," Osterlund said.

"Well, I'd be honored, sir," Dale said.

"I haven't asked you yet."

Dale slumped a little and caught his breath.

"You were driving a second-class car in that race today, but you drove it to win," Osterlund said.

"I always drive to win," Dale said.

"Every race?"

"Every race."

"Well, then, I guess you've answered my question," Osterlund said. He patted Dale on the back. "Nice meeting you, young lady."

He walked away from the table. Dale stared at his back.

"Dale Earnhardt!" Teresa whispered harshly. "Go after him!"

"Huh?"

"Go tell that man you won't wreck his car

if he puts you in the driver's seat!"

"But—"

"Don't you understand? Winston Cup isn't about winning every race—it's about getting the most points by the end of the year and winning the championship! That's what brings in the sponsors, and the money."

She was right of course, and he knew it. But he had told Osterlund the truth—driving to win was the only way he knew how to drive.

"Go after him!" she said. "Don't worry. We'll be right here." She put a hand on each child's shoulder, and they smiled.

He ran after Osterlund, catching up to him in the parking lot. "Look," he told the car owner. "I'll take care of your car, sir. I know you want that championship, and I know there's more than thirty races in the season. But I can't race my best if I don't go after the win every time. I can't race like you want me to if I'm worried about crashing."

Osterlund nodded slowly. "Let me think

about it," he said. "I'll call you when I decide."
Then he stuck out his hand for Dale to shake.
"Great race today, Dale."

Dale. He'd called him Dale.

Maybe there was a chance after all. . . .

Racing's New Star
1979

When it came, Osterlund's call changed Dale Earnhardt's life forever. For the entire next season, he would be competing on the Winston Cup Circuit!

It was the dream of a lifetime. Dale was thrilled—and anxious, too. The Winston Cup included not only oval-track races, but also a few road races, like the first one of the season, at Riverside Raceway in California.

Road races took place on the streets of cities, and you had to turn not only to the left, but also to the right. It was something Dale had never done.

But Rod Osterlund soothed his mind. He was going to invest in his driver the same way he had invested in his car and his team of mechanics—by going first-class all the way. He sent Dale to a special road-racing school in California for training.

He also helped Dale clean up his life—paying his debts for him, his bills and his child support payments. Osterlund was in the construction business, so he even built a house for Dale.

"How am I ever going to afford the payments on this place?" Dale wondered.

"That's why we're going to teach you how to live on a budget," Osterlund told him. He brought Dale over to his mansion to entertain him, and even let him drive his houseboat.

For Dale it was a whole new world. All the worries he'd been living with his whole life had been suddenly lifted from his shoulders.

All he had to do was concentrate on racing.

One of the best things Osterlund did was hire a top-notch team of veterans to back up his rookie driver. They were headed by crew chief Jake Ellert, a NASCAR legend.

Ellert and Dale became friends as they went over every detail of the car he would be driving that season. Ellert respected Dale's knowledge of the Monte Carlo's inner workings. He might have been just a rookie, but Earnhardt had been hanging around cars all his life, being taught by one of the best ever drivers—his daddy.

At Riverside Dale wasted no time showing the racing world the kind of stuff he was made of, making daring turns with two wheels on the infield grass, grazing the wall several times, and generally driving like the dirt-track madman he was. He fought his way up to tenth place by the finish. The rookie had arrived.

In race after race he would hit the wall,

bump into other cars, and pull off daredevil moves that had the other drivers hopping mad and jealous at the same time. They might have hated Dale for his aggressiveness, but they wished they could drive as fearlessly as he did.

"Speed didn't bother Dale," Roland Wlodyka would remember years later. "But there were a lot of other drivers who were scared to death of what he was doing."

In the seventh race of that season, the Volunteer 500 at Bristol, Dale's daring style and superb racing instincts paid off big-time. After two of the leaders wiped out in a crash, he swept into the lead and kept it for the final one hundred sixty laps, beating Bobby Allison by three seconds.

It was his first Winston Cup victory—only the fourth time in history a rookie driver had ever won a Winston Cup race—and Dale savored it, taking a victory lap that was as slow as any in memory.

"This is the big leagues," he said to the reporters who mobbed him in victory lane. He told them how he hoped his daddy was looking down on him and smiling. He wished Ralph could have been there to see it in person.

After that first win, Dale was sure there would soon be more to come. He nearly won in Texas before his tires blew out on the final laps.

But Dale's style of driving soon caught up with him. He'd been hard on the car all season—only an owner as rich and committed as Osterlund would have put up with a driver who caused so much damage to his car so often. But Dale had never considered the danger to *himself* in driving the way he did.

Then at Pocono Raceway in Pennsylvania it all caught up to him. His tire blew, and the car slammed into the wall so hard that Dale broke both his collarbones and suffered a concussion. Lucky to be alive, he was brought to the hospital by helicopter as the hushed crowd looked on.

That would have been the end of the season for most drivers—but not for Dale Earnhardt. It drove him crazy to be sidelined, and to have to watch while substitute driver David Pearson drove his car to victory at Darlington. Dale wondered whether Osterlund would be tempted to replace him with Pearson permanently. After all, Dale had cost the owner a lot of money for repairs. A more careful, cautious driver would be cheaper to keep.

He needn't have worried, though. Osterlund liked the way Dale went after the victory week after week, not caring what happened to him or the car along the way. The owner was sure he'd found the right driver. No substitute would take Dale's place for long.

Four weeks after his crash, Dale was back behind the wheel again. From that day forward, he never missed another Winston Cup race.

There were eight races left in the Winston Cup season that year, and Dale finished in the top ten in seven of them. When the dust cleared, he had come in seventh in the Winston Cup standings. He'd only won one race that year, but he'd had eleven top-five finishes.

Equally important, his earnings dwarfed anything he'd made before. In his first year on the big-league circuit, he made a whopping $264,086 for the Osterlund team. His share: more than $30,000.

For Dale it was an unimaginable amount of money. In his own mind, he was rich now beyond his wildest dreams. And his year was made even sweeter when he was voted Winston Cup Rookie of the Year over Harry Gant, Terry Labonte, and Joe Millikan in one of the closest rookie battles ever.

"I really believe this is only a start," Jake Ellert, the crew chief, said of Dale. "He's young and he's good. If he don't get hurt, he's got at least twelve good years ahead of him."

As it turned out, Ellert had nailed it right on the head.

The future looked bright. Dale's long, lonely road from nowhere had finally brought him within sight of NASCAR's mountaintop.

The next year, 1980, he would set his sights even higher—on the Winston Cup Championship itself.

Top of the World
1980

Rod Osterlund was not the only owner who thought Dale Earnhardt had the stuff to be a champion. That December Junior Johnson called to see if he'd like to switch teams and come drive a second car for him.

It was a tempting offer. Johnson's team was always in contention for the championship. Its number one-driver, Cale Yarborough, had won three of the last four seasons.

When Osterlund heard about it, he raced to offer Dale a five-year contract. Dale signed it. He was happy to have his future secured and to remain with the owner whose faith in him had made his incredible year possible.

The Osterlund team wasted no time getting to the top. In February 1980 at Daytona, NASCAR racing's premier speedway, Dale won the Busch Clash—a twenty-lap race among the previous year's twelve fastest drivers. His blue-and-yellow Chevy Monte Carlo with the white number 2 passed Darrell Waltrip on the outside on the final lap to win.

It was his first victory of the new season, although it didn't count in the season standings. The Clash was part of NASCAR's Busch Circuit—what used to be called the Sportsman Division until Busch decided to sponsor it. Still, it was a victory, with prize money attached.

"There might be a thing or two Richard Petty and Bobby Allison haven't shown me," the cocky young driver told reporters after the Busch Clash. "But I know I can run with the best of them."

There in victory lane to help Dale hoist the trophy was his girlfriend, Teresa. Unlike his ex-wives, she'd believed in him from the very beginning. She had stuck with him, encouraging him, through his darkest days. Now that he was a star in the making, she was there at his side, helping him keep his feet on the ground, even if his head was in the clouds.

In March at Atlanta Motor Speedway, he won the Atlanta 500, coming from thirty-first at the start to win after Cale Yarborough pulled out with ignition trouble in the final laps. It was the fifth race in a row where Dale had finished in the top five.

He made it six in a row by winning the Valleydale Southeastern 500 at Bristol—the second year in a row he'd won that race. Six races into the season and Dale already had three victories. More important, he was in first place in the race for the Winston Cup Championship!

There were changes to the team around him, though. Jake Ellert, known as "Suitcase" because he tended to switch teams every chance he got, left Osterlund suddenly. He was replaced by Doug Richert, a twenty-year-old member of the pit crew.

That made Dale nervous, even though he respected Richert for his knowledge of cars and their engines. Could the kid really replace the legend?

Osterlund reassured him. "Hey, a lot of people called *you* a kid not too long ago. Besides, I warned Doug about Jake leaving someday. He's been studying him all year, learning everything he can. He'll be all right—just give him a chance."

Even without Ellert, the team continued to do well. In July at the Busch Nashville 420, Dale beat off a furious charge from Cale Yarborough, who stood second in the season standings, to win the race. Yarborough bumped him several times during the last stages, but Dale Earnhardt was not someone who could be intimidated.

He won yet again at Martinsville in the Old Dominion 500. It was his fourth Winston Cup victory of the season—a record for a second-year driver.

Dale had a close call on the two hundred eighteenth lap, when his car was bumped and sent for a loop. Somehow, he managed to pull the car back into position without crashing. "It scared me," he admitted afterward. "I saw the inside wall, the outside wall, and then the racetrack. I said, 'Thank you, Lord.'"

The following week, he won yet again in the National 500 at Charlotte Motor Speedway, his home track. This time, he ran an almost perfect race to edge Cale Yarborough at the finish line. With only three races left in the season, he was still leading in the race for the Winston Cup Championship.

Then the call came.

He was at home, and Teresa was over, as she

usually was these days. She was his Carolina girlfriend. When he was on the road, he dated a lot of different women. Now that he was a winner the girls seemed to flock to his side. Dale liked all that attention, but there was something about Teresa he liked even more.

She was steady. She had common sense and a good education, too. She was great with his kids when they went out together on fishing trips. She was patient, never asking more from him than he was willing to give. And she had always believed in him—even when he wasn't sure he believed in himself.

He'd even thought about marrying her—but after two failed marriages and three kids he barely ever saw, he wasn't sure he wanted to go down that road again. Not yet, anyway.

When the phone rang. Dale went to pick it up. "Hello?"

"Dale? It's Brenda."

His ex-wife sounded terrible. Clearly, she was in tears. "The house . . . caught fire."

129

"What? Is everyone—?"

"We're all okay," she said, sniffing back tears. "But the whole place is gone. Bad kitchen wires, they said it was."

"Aw, gee, that's awful, Brenda. Do you need any help for the kids? I've got money now, I could—"

"The thing is, I'm not gonna be able to cope with them—not without a place for us to live," she said. "I was thinking . . . maybe they could come live with you for awhile."

"Aw, Brenda, I don't know . . ."

Teresa came up behind him. "It's okay, Dale. Let them come. They need their daddy now."

Dale covered the phone and turned to her. "Teresa, I don't know how to be a father to them. I hardly know what to do with them when I've got them on alternate weekends!"

"They need you now, Dale."

"And who's gonna be a mother to them?"

130

he asked her. "Who's gonna look after them when I'm on the road?"

She looked right into his eyes and said, "You leave that to me."

Teresa had graduated college and knew something about business. These days, she was studying up on corporations.

"You've got to have a corporation of your own, Dale," she told him one day, while eight-year-old Kelley and six-year-old Dale Jr. played in the living room. "You've got real money now and an image—and you've got to make sure they're protected."

"I don't know a thing about that," Dale admitted. "Why don't you just take charge of it? I trust you."

"Dale, we're not even married," she reminded him.

He felt bad about that. By now, he was pretty sure Teresa was the one for him—but he just wasn't ready to set a date yet. Right now, there was only one goal he was chasing—the NASCAR championship.

"You go ahead and get it set up," he said. "Now, what are we gonna call it?"

"I thought 'Dale Earnhardt, Inc.' sounded good," she said.

He laughed. "Yeah, that sure sounds like the name of a big corporation."

He didn't realize it at the time, but Dale Earnhardt, Inc. would grow to be a very big corporation indeed.

On the final weekend of the racing season, it all came down to a dogfight for the championship in Ontario, California, at the L.A. Times 500. The race turned out to be a duel between him and Cale Yarborough.

Dale led in the standings going into the race—and because he finished just two spots behind Yarborough in Ontario, Dale was the winner of the Winston Cup Championship— by a mere nineteen points!

It was the first time ever that a driver had won Rookie of the Year and then the championship in two consecutive years.

Just two years earlier, he had been broke and unknown. Now Dale Earnhardt was a champion, a star, and a man with some real money. The purse for the year was almost $600,000. A great year for Osterlund, and a very good first year for Dale Earnhardt, Inc.

Dale went off to celebrate in Las Vegas with his little brothers, staying in a huge suite. He was twenty-nine, newly rich, and had every reason to think he could win another championship the next year.

Having come this far this fast, it never occurred to Dale that things might not go so easily from here on in.

But the young, ragtag champion would be a middle-aged, married family man by the time he won the Winston Cup again.

Years of Change
1981–1983

Rod Osterlund was a man of many business interests. That winter his bankers told him he had to choose between racing and his development business.

He took their advice, and in June 1981, he sold his NASCAR team to a coal mining tycoon by the name of J. D. Stacy, who had no experience in racing.

Osterlund didn't have the heart to tell his team in person, so he called them from the West Coast. The news hit Dale like a brick.

Everyone on the team was angry. They'd

just won a championship! How could Oster-lund sell the team *now*?

Of course, that was just why Stacy had wanted to buy it. Now that he owned a cham-pionship team (as well as four other racing teams), he proceeded to hire a new head for the operation, Boobie Harrington.

Harrington, who knew nothing about rac-ing, immediately fired six members of the crew. After four more races, Dale left the team, taking his Wrangler sponsorship with him.

He was still driving well—in 1981 he racked up seventeen top-ten finishes out of thirty-one races. But he didn't win a single race that year, and he didn't grab a single pole position.

It was a terrible fall from the top, and it disappointed his fans as much as it did Dale.

Other team owners saw Dale's move from the Osterlund team as an opportunity to land one of the sport's hottest, most talented drivers. But most of them were committed to other drivers for the season.

One owner who wasn't was Richard Childress.

Childress had been a driver himself up to that time, building his own cars as well as racing them. He was just about broke, same as Dale had been two years earlier.

In fact, the two men were a lot alike— both were high school dropouts from the deep South, veterans of the dirt tracks. Childress had tangled with Dale plenty of times on the old Sportsman Circuit, but he'd never had the success Earnhardt had. In two hundred eighty-four races, he'd never won once.

In August of 1981 he'd just about reached the end of his rope. That was when he decided to stop driving, get a sponsor, and start his own team instead.

That happened to be the same weekend Dale decided to quit Stacy's team. He and

Childress ran into each other at the motel where they were both staying.

They both saw the possibilities of working together. With two sponsors—Wrangler and Goodyear (Childress's sponsor)—and a car that was ready to go, Dale wouldn't miss a beat.

More important, Childress was as committed to winning championships as Dale was. "My goal," Earnhardt's new boss said, "is to build indestructible cars that'll last a whole season's worth of races—and to put the roughest, hardest-driving, plain-old best driver in the world behind the wheel."

Dale laughed. "That'd be Richard Petty—he's not called The King for nothing. He's got seven Winston Cup Championships. I've got one."

"True, but I can't get Petty. Anyway, you look like the next best thing to me."

The two men agreed to give it a try. For the last ten races of 1981, Dale drove Childress's car, finishing in the top ten six times.

It was a good showing, but when the season was over, Childress advised Dale to sign with another team for the 1982 season. "Our team's not where we need to be yet," he told Dale. "It's a ten-year plan I'm working here. Right now, we're not close to championship caliber—and you need to be driving for the championship."

Dale felt bad about leaving Childress. They'd struck up a fast friendship. He appreciated the other man's honesty and generosity, and he knew Childress was right.

For the next two years, he would do his driving for Bud Moore's team, sponsored by Wrangler. Moore's team featured Fords, which Dale didn't like driving as well as the Chevys he had gotten used to with both Osterlund and Childress.

The Fords kept breaking down on him—in eighteen out of thirty races in 1982, Dale wasn't able to finish.

He did win the Rebel 500 at Darlington, edging Yarborough in a nip-and-tuck duel over the final laps, but that was his first victory in thirty-nine races, a losing streak the press fed on like a school of hungry sharks.

It was his only victory of 1982. He finished twelfth that year in the final standings. A disappointing showing, even though he had plenty of excuses—switching teams and crews, and having engines blow out on him time after time.

The following year featured more of the same. The yellow-and-blue Thunderbird with the blue number 15 won only two races that year and finished eighth in the Winston Cup standings.

Meanwhile, Richard Childress had continued to perfect his cars, using Ricky Rudd as his driver.

Rudd was a good racer, but more than that, he was a good communicator. He would test out every new twist in a car and report back to the team of mechanics and engineers, going into great detail. With Rudd's help, Childress's cars were getting better fast. The ten-year plan was quickly becoming a five-year plan.

Talking over the fine points of engine and drive-train performance was not something Dale could have done. He was not a talker, never had been.

In fact, even now, when he got in front of the press, or when he was around educated people, he tended to just keep his mouth shut. He had never forgotten that he'd dropped out of school in ninth grade.

Dale kept track of developments on the Childress team. He remembered how well he and Childress had clicked. He remembered their deal too.

Ricky Rudd was doing about as well as Dale. He finished ninth in 1982, and again in 1983, winning two races that year, the same number as Dale.

The thing Dale most admired about the Childress cars was that they were built from scratch. Every single part was custom-made. Nothing was store-bought. Nobody else in NASCAR was doing that.

Dale sure hoped Childress didn't go broke before the two of them got back together.

In June of 1982 Dale took official custody of Kelley and Dale Jr. His ex-wife Brenda was having a hard time financially. She'd lost her house and needed to work long hours.

Of course, Dale didn't have much time for the kids either. Teresa had to look after them while he was away racing. She was doing a great job too—both kids loved her.

This seemed to Dale to be as good a time as any to get married. He'd been in another bad crash at Pocono and fractured his kneecap. He raced the next week anyway, then checked himself into the hospital. That's where he was when he popped the question to Teresa.

They were married on November 14. For the first time in his life, Dale had a stable existence—a wife and children, a house, and a successful career.

Thinking back as he stood before the preacher with Teresa's hand in his, Dale could feel the hurt and anger draining out of him—the same hurt and anger that had made him such a terror on the race track.

Oh he would still be a terror out there— more than ever. But never again would he be reckless in his personal life. He would rely on Teresa, his rock, to keep things steady from now on.

She would never disappoint him. Teresa proved to be an extremely shrewd business-woman, as well as an excellent stepmom. She now took over formally as president of Dale Earnhardt, Inc. and immediately began to manage everything from Dale's image to his diet (she made sure he ate healthful foods

142

and didn't ruin his health with a lot of junk food).

Dale was happy with her—happier than he'd ever been in his life. In fact, the only place where things weren't going well for him was on the track. He was making enough money to live on, but he wasn't winning.

At the end of the 1983 season, he and Richard Childress met to discuss their future together.

"How's it coming?" Dale asked him.

"Much better'n I had any right to expect," Childress said.

"You ready for me to step in?" Dale asked. "Cause I'm ready to bolt and come on over."

"What about sponsorship?" Childress wondered. "I've got Frontier Airways backing me, but if we're gonna win a championship, we're gonna need a lot more money, and that means another sponsor. You think Wrangler would come over with you?"

Dale shook his head. "I don't know. Let me

put Teresa on the case. She's pretty sharp."

In the end, Wrangler decided to back both Bud Moore's team and Childress's. For the 1984 season, Dale and Ricky Rudd switched rides, with Rudd going into Moore's car.

As for Dale Earnhardt, he would drive the number 3 car for Richard Childress straight to immortality.

Together, the two would achieve phenomenal success and help transform NASCAR into a major national sport.

The Road to the Top
1984–1986

"The best thing about Dale Earnhardt was that he loved winning car races more than anything else in life. The grin on his face when he won said it all."

Those were the words of Kirk Shelmerdine, crew chief of the Childress team when Dale first took the wheel of car number 3 in 1984.

Dale was thirty-three years old, in his prime years as a race car driver. Shelmerdine was only twenty-two, but he'd had success with Ricky Rudd the past two years, and Dale had confidence in him.

For his part, Shelmerdine was a big fan of Dale's. "He was one ill son of a gun when he went on that track. You couldn't ask for anything more from a driver."

In 1984, his first full year with Childress, Dale won only two races. But he finished in the top five twelve times, and in the top ten twenty-two times. It was good enough for a fourth-place finish in the Winston Cup standings at the end of the year.

In 1985, his second year behind the wheel of the blue-and-yellow Chevy Monte Carlo, Dale was feeling more comfortable and took even more risks.

He wasn't afraid to use fenders and bumpers to shove other cars out of his way. NASCAR's "bad boy" wound up taking out Tim Richmond in three separate races that year. Richmond swore he'd get even, but he never was able to muster the nerve to trade paint with Dale.

146

Needless to say, Richmond wasn't the only driver who didn't like Dale very much. Winston Cup champion Darrell Waltrip said, "I guess NASCAR thinks that over-aggressive driving sells tickets." When reporters asked who he meant, he pointed to Dale's number 3 car. "Y'all know who to watch if that's what you want to see."

But Dale didn't care if the other drivers liked him. "No one gives you anything in this life," he said, "so that means you have to go out there and make it happen for yourself."

And his style did sell tickets. Love him or hate him, people came to the racetrack to see Dale. Some of them showered boos on him every time he came around the track. Some even threw their drinks at him.

But Dale did have a dedicated, even fanatical base of fans. They loved him because he was fearless, rough, and fierce—just like they wanted to be, even if they weren't. They loved him because he was down-home, an underdog with no education and no money, but with a will to win like no other.

And they bought his souvenirs! Earnhardt merchandise was sold at the track for the first time in 1985, from the back of a trailer. That year, Dale's share of the souvenir take was more than one hundred eighty thousand dollars! It was an incredible sum, but it was nothing compared to what was to come.

In time most NASCAR fans would be won over to Earnhardt's side—but that would take time, and another championship, to accomplish.

Unfortunately for Dale, he wound up wrecking or unable to finish eleven times in 1985. He won four races, although he had fewer top-five and top-ten finishes than the year before, and finished only eighth in the standings.

His victories were all on short tracks of less than a mile, the kind he used to race on back in the old days—the kind his daddy had raced on too.

But NASCAR was growing rapidly, and more and more of the Winston Cup tracks being built around the country were super-speedways with long straightaways that let drivers achieve incredible speeds.

Dale would have to bring home some victories on those longer tracks in 1986—and avoid wrecking so often—if he expected to win a second championship.

In April 1986, Dale Earnhardt turned thirty-five years old. He was now officially middle-aged. He had a wife, two children, a nice home, and what was beginning to be a pretty hefty pile of money put away.

He had a contract, a fine sponsor, an owner he liked, and good friends.

But he hadn't won since 1980. He'd gone five years without a championship. He wasn't about to go a sixth.

The NASCAR season begins with a full week of races at Daytona. First there's

Speed Week—a series of shorter contests, going fewer laps. Then there's the fifty-lap Busch Clash and the International Race of Champions—the first of four IROC races in a NASCAR year. In these races, all the drivers race identical cars that differ only in color and number.

Finally, there are the qualifiers—one hundred twenty-five-lap races that determine where in the pack the racers will start the week's final race—Winston Cup's biggest—the Daytona 500.

Dale had been in the big race seven times before—he'd come in second two years back when he couldn't get past Cale Yarborough, but he'd never won.

This year he meant to kick off the season right, by taking home stock car racing's biggest single prize.

He began by winning the Busch Clash. Four days later, he won the one hundred twenty-five-mile qualifier. The buzz around the great speedway grew louder—Earnhardt looked good to take all the marbles this time.

He went into the 500 as the favorite. Near the end of the race he looked unstoppable as he came up alongside leader Geoffrey Bodine. Running only an inch or so behind Bodine with three laps to go, Dale was perfectly positioned to slingshot by him into the lead.

Then, suddenly, Dale's engine started sputtering.

Oh, no! He'd run out of gas!

He had to pit and gas up, and wound up finishing fourteenth. It was a huge disappointment, but Dale took it in stride. "I can take losing, just like I can take winning," he told the press.

There would be plenty of other chances to win the big race. Besides, Dale had bigger fish to fry—there was a Winston Cup to win!

Meanwhile things were changing fast on

the family front. In 1986 Dale's first child, Kerry, walked back into his life. He was old enough now to strike out on his own, and he had decided he wanted to be a race car driver—or at least an auto mechanic. Dale and Teresa welcomed the sixteen-year-old into their home.

Kelley and Dale Jr. had never even met their half brother, but the three of them quickly became friends. Soon they were out at the go-kart track, racing each other while their father looked on proudly.

"You know," Dale said to Teresa, who stood by his side, "I think Kelley's the one with the most talent of the three. If she were a boy, she could be a pro."

It was too bad, he thought. The racing world, always dominated by men, was not yet ready to accept women as drivers, or even on pit crews.

Kelley might someday drive in "powder-puff derbies," as they called ladies' races.

After all, Dale's mother, Martha, had done it, and so had his sisters. But Kelley would never race for NASCAR.

As for the boys, Dale Jr. showed some racing talent, but what really set him apart was his grit and toughness. After a particularly bad crash one time, the twelve-year-old boy lay on the ground in pain—but all he wanted to know was where his go-kart was, and if it was okay.

"That was the only thing he was concerned about," Dale remembered later. "It was pretty awesome."

It was the first inkling of what lay ahead for Dale Earnhardt Jr.—a brilliant NASCAR career of his own that continues to this day.

Dale was pleased that all three of his kids wanted to take after their daddy. But he was not around much, and he felt it would be better for Kelley and Dale Jr. if they went to military school for a while. He thought it might provide some of the discipline he couldn't give them.

153

The kids didn't like the idea, but later they both agreed it helped them mature.

Dale's fast start in 1986 made everyone sit up and take notice. It looked like the new season would feature Earnhardt and last season's winner, smooth-as-silk Darrell Waltrip.

Waltrip was no fan of Dale's. Over the course of the year, he sometimes made rude comments about him to the press. "I'd put some psychological stuff in the papers," he said, "but it wouldn't do any good, 'cause Dale and his boys can't read."

When reporters told Dale what Waltrip had said about him, he replied, "I can read. Just like in a kid's early reader. See Darrell run his mouth. See Darrell fall."

Dale's daddy had taught him that the place to duke it out was not in the press but on the track. At Richmond Raceway, he ran Waltrip right into the wall, wrecking both their cars with only three laps to go in the race. The two

154

men nearly came to blows afterward and had to be separated.

All year long Dale kept his focus on the big prize. He won in April at Darlington for his first victory of the season, dominating the race from start to finish.

He won again the next week at Wilkesboro, just barely beating Ricky Rudd in the car he himself had driven the year before.

The fans and the press were already calling it the "Year of Dale Earnhardt." For years they'd watched in awe as he pulled amazing moves out of his hat in race after race. Now, it seemed, all the elements were coming together for him.

But Darrell Waltrip wasn't going to give up his crown without a fight. The points race between the two was close the entire season, but Dale stayed in the lead most of the way.

He won the biggest race of his career, the Coca-Cola 600, at Charlotte in May. It was the race he'd watched his daddy run, standing in the back of the truck all those years ago. Now, with his home-town fans cheering him on, he gave them what they wanted—a victory.

He won there again in October, and came into the season's second-to-last race, in Atlanta, needing only to come in tenth to clinch the championship.

Dale did better than that—he won the race outright.

For the second time, he was the Winston Cup champion!

He gave all the credit to Richard Childress and the Wrangler team. "It was Richard's effort that built the team and put it in the position it is in today," he said.

But it was Dale who had driven the car. He was the face of the team, and now he was a genuine NASCAR superstar!

The Intimidator
1987–1994

Dale's earnings for 1986 totaled more than 1.7 million dollars—almost four times what he'd earned in any previous year. He'd thought he was rich then—but now?

And this was only the beginning.

Teresa was the first to see what this second championship really meant. Under her watchful eye, Dale Earnhardt, Inc. was about to start making tens of millions of dollars a year, most of it off the track.

NASCAR had grown a lot since Dale's first cup win in 1980 and was now ready to explode onto the national scene. Dale had become champion at just the right time. He was fast becoming NASCAR's new superstar—the face of racing, just when the sport was hitting its stride.

He was controversial, daring, and tough—the very image NASCAR wanted to project to its fans. The leaders of the sport could only hope Dale would continue to lead the pack in the coming years.

He did not disappoint them—although he still didn't win the Daytona 500 in 1987.

His first win of the year came in the Goodwrench 500 in March, by a whopping eleven seconds.

The following week he won again, the day after he'd nearly wrecked his car in a practice run (the Childress team somehow got it back in shape for the race).

He won for a third time in March when Bill Elliott, the leader, ran out of gas just a couple of turns from the finish line at Darlington.

Earlier in the race, Dale's Chevy had hit the wall hard, but he'd somehow managed to keep the damaged car going.

By the time the first eight races of the season were over, Dale had won six of them! By the end of April, there was no longer any doubt that he would win his second straight Winston Cup championship.

But there was still a lot of racing to do. And on May 17, in the Winston, an all-star shootout race, Dale pulled a move that is still remembered to this day as the "Pass in the Grass."

After Bill Elliott had dominated the two qualifying rounds, everyone was looking forward to the day's grand finale—a ten-lap race for the trophy.

On the very first lap, Elliott and Geoff Bodine bumped, and Dale took advantage to burst past the two of them into the lead.

Elliott, convinced it was Dale who'd bumped him, took off after him. The two of them bumped each other back and forth for the next few laps. At one point, Elliott rode Dale into the infield grass on the inside of the track.

Normally, that would have been the end of it. It's impossible to drive on grass as fast as on asphalt and still keep control of the car.

But somehow, Dale did it. He kept the car in a straight line, at top speed, and reemerged onto the asphalt one hundred fifty feet later, alone in first place!

One lap later Dale ran Elliott into the wall. Afterward Dale claimed there'd been no contact. Elliott insisted Dale had bumped him.

Either way, it caused damage that made Elliott's tire blow out. He had to pit and wound up finishing in fourteenth place.

Fuming, Elliott and Geoff Bodine both bumped Dale during his victory lap after the race. Elliott also tried to cut him off several times. He and Dale and their teams nearly came to blows in the pit afterward.

"If a man has to run over you to beat you, it's time to stop," Elliott complained to the press. "This is not Saturday night wrestling."

But although it may have made him another enemy in Bill Elliott, the "Pass in the Grass" made Dale Earnhardt a hero to millions of racing fans.

He was no longer just an overaggressive driver in their eyes. He was a working-class hero, fighting against the powers-that-be for all he was worth, trying to get to the top of the heap by any means necessary.

After the "Pass in the Grass," Dale earned a new nickname, one that would stick with him for the rest of his life. No longer was he called Ironhead. From 1987 on, Dale Earnhardt was known as "The Intimidator."

He won eleven of twenty-nine races that year, for his third Winston Cup Championship, and his second in a row. In December, he was voted Driver of the Year by the National Motorsports Press Association for the first time.

Along with his new nickname, he and the number 3 car were about to get a new sponsor, and a whole new image. Wrangler was bought by another company that didn't want to sponsor NASCAR—and into the void stepped GM Goodwrench. They agreed to back the Childress team. For the rest of Dale's life, he, Childress, and Goodwrench would be a team.

The new sponsor wanted a new look, and Dale and Teresa liked it right away. No longer would the number 3 car be yellow and blue. From now on, it would be jet black. Dale would look the part of the Intimidator too, wearing mirrored sunglasses and looking tough as nails.

The Intimidator in look as well as driving style.

Racing's Darth Vader.

The new image was a major hit with fans, who bought millions of dollars worth of merchandise. Dale Earnhardt, Inc. kept control of all merchandising contracts, under Teresa's watchful eye.

Other corporations looked on in envy. Time after time over the next few years, they would try to convince Dale and Teresa to bolt the Childress team and start their own, with different sponsorship of course.

But their efforts were in vain. While Dale did eventually start his own racing team, he himself continued to drive for Childress, staying true to the man who'd always stood by him.

For Dale Earnhardt, loyalty was not negotiable.

In the summer of 1987, Kerry and Dale Jr. began working on a '78 Monte Carlo to prepare it for racing.

Dale Sr. had to laugh. Kerry was seventeen, and Dale Jr. was twelve—they were still a few years from driving a race car, but they sure seemed to be serious about it.

Dale made sure the car had all the latest

safety features, then let them keep working. Years later the three kids would alternate weeks on the dirt tracks, then compare notes on who drove the best. The common opinion was that Kerry was reckless and crashed too much and that Kelley was the most talented.

Dale eventually bought them each a car to race.

Kerry would continue driving until he had a wife and kids of his own. He still does some racing as of this writing.

Kelley kept at it for a while too, but she just couldn't convince enough guys to work on a car for a girl driver. Finally, she gave up in frustration.

It was Dale Jr. who went the furthest and followed in his father's footsteps, ten years after those first go-kart races.

With all the money being invested in the Childress/Earnhardt operation by GM Good-wrench, the company expected Dale to attend

a lot of sponsor events. But Dale was not an easy horse to tame. Time after time, he'd blow off an event to go hunting or fishing with Neil Bonnett.

Dale was thrilled when Bonnett started off the 1988 season by winning the second and third races—especially since he'd crashed so badly the year before that his doctors said he'd be out for a year. (Try twelve weeks—like Dale, Neil Bonnett was one tough hombre!)

That year, Dale finished third in the NASCAR standings, with three wins and thirteen top-five finishes. More important, he and Teresa had a daughter of their own, Taylor Nicole. Now there were four Earnhardt children under the family roof.

In 1989 Dale won five times, with fourteen top-five finishes. He ended up losing the championship to Rusty Wallace by only twelve points—the closest finish in Winston Cup history. Dale won the last race of the year, in Atlanta, and Wallace finished fifteenth—just good enough to win the Cup.

Afterward Dale shrugged it off. His team was rounding back into form after a two-year slump. "Watch out for 1990," he warned the rest of the NASCAR field. "Right now, I'm going hunting."

Neil Bonnett was just getting out of the hospital—he'd broken his sternum in a crash in August. Now, once again, the two friends went off in search of solitude and nature, away from the bustle of reporters, sponsors, and fans.

There, out in the woods, Dale had time to think about the future—and about a big event that had happened a few years earlier— Ralph Earnhardt's induction into the National Motorsports Press Association Hall of Fame. (Later both he and Dale would be voted among their fifty greatest drivers of all time.)

● ● ●

In 1990 the Childress team had one goal—to climb back to the top and reclaim the cup they hadn't won for two straight years. If you had told them then that they were about to win the cup in four out of the next five years, they would have laughed and called you crazy.

But they did.

Childress's ten-year plan had come to fruition in just five years. But after recovering from its initial surprise, the racing world had slowly caught up.

Things were no longer as they were in 1986 and 1987, when the Childress team's cars and their precision engineering were at the cutting edge of racing science.

The year 1990 began with a huge disappointment at the Daytona 500. Dale was leading the race with less than a mile to go, and the crowd was going wild—The Intimidator was finally going to win the one big race he'd never been able to conquer.

And then fate struck again in the form of

a small piece of metal that cut one of Dale's rear tires. The tire fell apart on him, and he wound up coming in a heartbreaking fifth.

After the race he sat alone in the car for several minutes. No one dared come near him. Everyone knew how he felt.

After that day the jinx talk began in earnest. Would Earnhardt *ever* win the big one? Or would it be the one race that truly beat him?

Mark Martin, it turned out, was the driver to beat in 1990. Dale trailed him all year but never fell out of the race for the championship.

Along the way, Dale won at Atlanta (twice), Darlington (twice), Talladega (twice), Charlotte, Michigan, Daytona (the Pepsi 400), and Richmond.

The Richmond race was the second-to-last of the season, and Dale came out of it with a six-point lead over Martin going into the year's final race at Atlanta.

Dale came in third there, ahead of Martin, and won the cup by twenty-six points, capping off an incredible year with nine victories, eighteen top five finishes, and three million dollars in prize money—more than any driver had ever earned in a single year!

His off-the-track earnings were a lot higher than that.

"Used to be, you didn't think much about the fan," Dale told an interviewer. "He bought a ticket and he was up there sitting in the stands. But in Greenville on Labor Day, there were about eight thousand people there, and there might have been one out of a hundred who didn't have something on that said Earnhardt."

It was Dale's fourth Winston Cup Championship, the second-most ever behind Richard Petty's seven titles. People were saying that Dale was still young enough to catch The King. But Dale always said that Petty was the greatest ever.

• • •

The following winter, when Dale was presented with his Winston Cup trophy at NASCAR's annual dinner, his mother, Martha, was able to attend for the first time. It was an especially important moment for Dale, who said, "Her being here means a lot to me. I just wish Daddy could have been too, because he has never left my heart."

He also spoke about dropping out of high school (Kelley and Dale Jr. were now back in public schools and living at home): "I've made sure my kids don't make the same mistake I did," he said. "I think an education would have helped me a lot, both from the sponsor side and the fan side of it. I've had to rely on a lot of common sense and good advice from my wife, Teresa."

Dale had grown up a lot in the past few years. He'd settled down and become a family man, with a big house on Lake Norman, a country farm, and a Chevy dealership.

171

He still took chances out on the track, but now he was smoother and more calculating. It was as if a part of his daddy had awakened inside him and made him an even better racer.

Another big change in Dale's life took place in August of that year, when Neil Bonnett had a terrible accident on the track.

He was hurt so badly that, when he first woke up in the hospital, he had complete amnesia. The very first memory that came back to him was of hunting with Dale out in the woods.

Neil's doctors said he'd most likely never race again. That hit Neil incredibly hard.

Dale had to help him through it. "You've got to get back out there," he told his friend. "It's what you love. It's what your life's all about."

He might as well have been talking about himself. But Neil's accident had affected Dale as well. For the first time, it really hit home that he could get killed out there.

The knowledge didn't stop him, or even slow him down—but it was always there, from that moment on. He carried it with him in his heart, defying fate at two hundred miles per hour, for the rest of his life.

The next year, 1991, started about the same as 1990 had—Dale was leading the Daytona with two laps to go, when he and Davey Allison spun out. Dale wound up finishing fifth, and the monkey on his back got a little heavier.

He was about to turn forty. How many more cracks at NASCAR's Super Bowl would he have?

Dale won only four times that year—at Richmond, Martinsville, Talladega, and North Wilkesboro—and finished in the top five fourteen times—but it was enough to win an incredible fifth Winston Cup title.

It wasn't that Dale raced especially well

that year—or that the Childress cars were the best in the field (they weren't any more—the cars put together by Ed Roush had overtaken them). But all the other drivers in contention early dropped off as the season went along, and the ones who made a late charge fell short of catching him.

Would 1992 make it three years in a row? Only Cale Yarborough had achieved that feat.

Dale looked good going in—but a crash in the Daytona 500 set the tone for the entire year. It was a bad year for the Childress team in general.

With Neil Bonnett watching from the broadcast booth, where he now worked while recovering from his injuries, Dale won only once—in the year's longest race, the Coca-Cola 600—and came in a dismal (for him) twelfth in the year-end standings.

Kirk Shelmerdine, Childress's crew chief through all the glory years, decided he'd had

174

enough and quit to go follow his childhood dream of being a dirt-track racer. To replace him for the 1993 season, Childress lured Andy Petree away from the Leo Jackson/Harry Gant team.

With all the turmoil, and the subpar 1992, not many people expected Dale to roar back for a sixth championship in 1993.

Yet he did.

After another huge disappointment in the Daytona 500—he was passed on the last lap by Dale Jarrett and came in second—he went on to win six of the first eighteen Winston Cup races.

And he was still driving his competitors crazy.

In the Charlotte 600 he needed a caution flag to stay in the lead (under the caution flag, no driver can pass another). So while lapping a slower driver, Greg Sacks, Dale ran him across the track and into the wall. Out came the yellow caution flag, and Dale's lead was secure for the rest of the race.

In 1993 NASCAR had an awful year. In April reigning Winston Cup champ Alan Kulwicki was killed in a plane crash. Soon afterward Davey Allison lost his life when his helicopter went down.

The whole racing world went into mourning. A month later, after the race at Pocono, all the drivers knelt in prayer for their lost comrades.

Then Dale did a victory lap, circling the track the wrong way in honor of Kulwicki, while holding a flag with Allison's number 28 out his window in tribute.

The crowd cheered and cheered.

The next weekend featured another victory for Dale at the Diehard 500 at Talladega. It also marked Neil Bonnett's return to racing, one and a half years after his head injury.

Driving Dale's backup car, Bonnett crashed badly in the race—but was uninjured. Dale, and everyone else, breathed a huge sigh of relief.

After those first six victories, Dale didn't win another race all year. In the final race of 1993, Dale finished tenth, just good enough to hold off Rusty Wallace's charge and win an incredible sixth Winston Cup Championship!

Richard Petty and his record seven titles were now in sight.

As the new year dawned, Dale Earnhardt was beginning to be called by yet another nickname—The Dominator.

And dominate he did in 1994, running away from the field. He won only four times, but he came in second seven times and third six times. It was enough to secure the championship with two races still to go in the season.

Seven championships! From now on King Richard would have to share his record and his throne with Dale Earnhardt.

And although Dale would always deny it,

pointing to Petty's untouchable two hundred-plus victories, many people have referred to Dale Earnhardt ever since as the greatest race car driver who ever lived.

That year, 1994, should have been great for Dale Earnhardt, and in many ways it was. He won the preliminary races at Daytona (the Busch Clash for the sixth straight year and the one hundred twenty-five-mile qualifier for the fifth straight time). He won his seventh championship, tying Petty, and his winnings totaled more than three million dollars for the second year in a row.

But the year had no sooner begun than it was marred by a terrible tragedy. On February 11, Neil Bonnett was doing a practice run at Daytona, alone on the track, when his car rammed the wall, killing him.

Years before Dale and Neil had made a pact not to attend each other's funerals. So Dale didn't go. Instead, he grieved the loss of his best friend in the only way he knew how—he prayed for him, then went back out the next weekend and won a race in his honor.

He stood there in victory lane, with his friend's name painted in bold letters on the side of his car. "I miss my buddy," he said. "I miss him being here for the good times, and I miss him giving me hell over the bad times. I do the same things I always did, but none of it feels the same. I'm just going to keep on winning. That's the best way I know to pay tribute."

It was the worst loss Dale had suffered since the death of his daddy. But he never let himself cry until that seventh Winston Cup was his. Only then did he let the tears flow.

With Bonnett's death, Dale was more aware than ever that everything he had could be lost in an instant. One mistake on the track, one moment of bad judgment—yours or someone else's—could mean injury or death.

Other men might have hung up their helmets

then and there. With seven championships Dale certainly didn't have much left to prove. There was a potential eighth championship, to be sure. And he'd never won the Daytona 500. But in the end, what convinced Dale to keep racing was that it was the only life he knew. Racing was him, and he was racing.

And so, he soldiered on, in his friend's memory.

Crashing and Burning
1995–1997

In 1995 NASCAR saw the birth of a great new rivalry—Jeff Gordon versus Dale Earnhardt. Gordon had come along in 1993 and won Rookie of the Year, impressing everyone with his style as well as his driving skills.

It was a natural rivalry in many ways. Dale wore black; Gordon preferred rainbow colors. Dale was an unsophisticated country boy; Gordon had polish and leading-man looks. Dale was gruff and shy; Gordon was the darling of the press. When Dale won, he drank champagne; When Gordon won, he drank milk.

Fans quickly split into two camps. You could root for Dale or Gordon, but not ever for both.

The year began with yet another bitter disappointment for Dale at the Daytona 500. He put a late charge on Sterling Marlin, but came up just short, finishing second.

He wound up coming in second for the year as well, losing the championship to Gordon (by a mere thirty-four points) even though he won five races, had nineteen top five finishes, and won more than three million dollars for the third year in a row.

Dale was disappointed that he'd come so close to breaking Richard Petty's record of seven titles and yet fallen short. But he realized that Jeff Gordon was no fluke (as of this writing, Gordon has four Winston Cup titles under his belt).

Dale started 1996 in fine fashion, winning the Daytona qualifier for the seventh straight year, then coming in second in the 500 for the second straight time (he couldn't quite get past Dale Jarrett on the final lap).

The jinx talk grew even louder. But Dale had no time to dwell on it—there were other races to be run, and won.

The following week he won at North Carolina, and then was victorious at Atlanta in March. Talk of an eighth title was the buzz at every track.

Then, on July 28 at Talladega, with Dale trailing by only twelve points in the Winston Cup standings, everything changed in an instant.

In the lead on lap one hundred seventeen, on a rain-slicked track, his car was bumped from behind, causing a horrific crash that sent number 3 into the wall, breaking Dale's sternum. The number 3 car ended up on its side.

Car after car smashed into his, breaking Dale's collarbone as well. The crash was so bad that two other drivers were killed.

Everyone was sure Dale had to be dead as well.

The emergency squad was about to cut open the roof of Dale's car to get him out, but he waved them off and, in great pain, climbed out on his own.

"Just walk me to the ambulance," he told them, and somehow made it there on his own, to the thunderous cheers of the crowd.

Even more incredibly, when the next race took place at Watkins Glen two weeks later, he was back behind the wheel. Not only that, he won the pole position as the fastest qualifying car and came in sixth in the race!

NASCAR fans were astonished. They yelled their lungs out in support of the bravest driver they'd ever seen.

Dale raced in pain for the rest of that season, but his injuries obviously affected his performance. The departure of crew chief Andy Petree at the end of 1995 also contributed to a disappointing fourth-place finish for the year.

Still, it was one of Dale's most impressive years on the track. To do as well as he had, and not miss a single race, while hurt that badly was astonishing.

After all, he could easily have quit. Losing Neil and getting seriously injured, all in the space of one year, might have made other drivers think about retiring.

Dale was forty-five years old now. He had two grandchildren. He had won more than thirty million dollars in prize money and earned a whole lot more from endorsements and merchandising. He'd built a huge shop in front of his lakefront home that was so big it was nicknamed the "Garage Mahal," after the famous and enormous monument in India, the Taj Mahal.

He had a yacht named *Sunday Money*, because that's what had paid for it. He had another huge boat, and a private jet, too. There was the Chevy dealership, the farm, and now even a racing team of his own.

It would have been easy for him to hang up his helmet.

But there were still a few things Dale Earnhardt wanted to accomplish. There was, of course, that eighth championship. There was the Daytona 500. And now there was the prospect of racing against his son Dale Jr.

Junior had made great progress, and in 1996 he was driving short-track along with Kelley and Kerry. But Dale Jr. was doing so well that he was about to graduate to NASCAR's Busch Circuit.

If his daddy could hang around for another couple of years, they might find themselves on the same track together.

Earnhardt began 1997 with another victory in the one hundred twenty-five-mile qualifier during Speed Week at Daytona—his eighth straight win in the race.

But that turned out to be Dale's only victory that year.

In the Daytona 500 he was running second, with eleven laps to go. He was ready to make his move, when he collided with eventual winner Jeff Gordon. Dale's car went flying, rolling over and spinning until it was a mangled wreck.

Dale got out and was being walked to the ambulance when he looked back at the car. "Man, the wheels ain't knocked off yet," he said.

He turned around, got back into the car, and, incredibly, started racing again. He finished in a distant thirty-first, but his courage stirred everyone who saw it.

Nothing, it seemed, could stop Dale Earnhardt.

But with rotating crew chiefs, lots of turnover on the team, a still-hurting driver, and a new crop of competitors, it was harder to win the cup than ever.

Another accident later that year aggravated Dale's injuries from the crash at Talladega the year before. He was in so much pain that he had to get out of the car in mid-race and, for the first time in his entire career, let a substitute driver finish the race for him.

Then, in the first lap of a race at Talladega that autumn, he started seeing double behind the wheel. Overcome by dizziness, he hit the wall twice and missed pit road once before finally getting safely off the track. No sooner had he stopped the car than he passed out cold.

For several days, while twenty-five different doctors ran tests to find out what had happened, Dale worried that he might not ever be able to race again. After all, his daddy had died of a heart attack at age forty-five.

Dale was already forty-six.

When the tests came back normal, the doctors decided it was a migrainelike episode and would probably never happen again. Dale was relieved, of course, but he was also more determined than ever to win that eighth Winston Cup Championship.

During the time he thought he might die, Dale realized how much he loved racing. He knew then that he wanted to keep doing it for as long as he could stay competitive.

And he was certain he could still compete. He wound up coming in fifth that year, despite everything.

With new crew chief Larry McReynolds firmly in place, the future looked good for the Childress team.

Sure enough, 1998 provided one of the highlights of Dale Earnhardt's illustrious career—perhaps his greatest moment as a race car driver.

Daytona
1998

People had been wondering since his 1996 accident at Talladega whether Dale would ever get back to being on top. Going into Daytona in February 1998, he had a fifty-nine–race losing streak going (not counting qualifiers).

And of course, when he won the qualifier again, for the ninth straight time, people shrugged it off. He'd already won thirty races at Daytona International Speedway—more than any other driver in the history of the track.

It was his twentieth Daytona 500. He'd come in second three of the past five years. He'd come so close so many times. The press, the fans, the other drivers—they all loved to ask about the jinx.

Sure, he'd go into the 500 as the favorite to win, just like he did every year. And just like every year, something would happen, probably on the last lap, to keep him from winning the big race.

Two nights before the race, at a large dinner where several drivers spoke, Buddy Baker and Darrell Waltrip joked about the jinx.

When it was Dale's turn to speak he said, "It just makes me want to go out there and dominate on Sunday. Then we'll have to get all these guys back together again next year so I can bring my trophy with me and polish it up in front of them."

On the eve of the race Dale was troubled. His team had had to replace the entire engine that day, and he wasn't sure the new one

191

would work properly. That's when he ran into the daughter of the track's owner. She told him that some very sick children had asked to meet with him through the Make-A-Wish Foundation. Would he come and visit them now?

Dale had always gone to see sick children— he never brought the press along with him, though. He didn't want the world to see his tenderhearted side. That would have only weakened his tough image in the world's eyes, and he wasn't going to let that happen.

But in private he could be as softhearted as anyone. That night, as he recalled later, "One little girl in a wheelchair gave me a penny and said, 'I rubbed this penny, and it's going to win you the Daytona 500. It's your race.'"

At the track the next morning, Dale glued the lucky penny onto his dashboard. He then tucked a small stuffed animal under his racing suit and, on command, started his engine.

He had already done a lot of mental work

to put himself in the right frame of mind. The month before he'd watched John Elway and the Denver Broncos win the Super Bowl after losing four times.

"If Elway can do it," he told himself, "so can I."

Dale was in the thick of things from the very start of the race. He held the lead four times, and lost it each time. Then, on lap one hundred forty out of two hundred, he took the lead a fifth time.

By then his chief rival, Jeff Gordon, had fallen out of contention when his tire was cut on a piece of metal. This time, it looked like the jinx had changed its target.

For the final sixty laps of the race, Dale held the lead. The whole time, the crowd held its breath as driver after driver came up behind him and tried to get by.

He held them all off one after another.

As he came into the final two laps with the lead, everyone was wondering what piece of bad luck would cost Dale the victory this time. But the good luck penny must have been working overtime.

Just before the final lap there was an accident in back of the pack, and the yellow caution flag came out. When Dale raced by it in first place, it meant all he had to do was get around the track one more time, and the victory would be his.

He prayed that his car wouldn't fall apart underneath him. It didn't. He cruised to the greatest victory of his career, and then in sheer joy did figure-eights all over the infield lawn. But he did them in such a way that it wrote a number 3 for all the world to see.

"I'm pretty good at writin', huh?" he yelled.

The crowd went wild. And as Dale rolled onto pit road, all the crews from all the racing teams he'd been competing against so fiercely all these years lined up to solemnly shake his hand. It was an awesome tribute to

195

racing's greatest competitor, and perhaps its greatest driver ever.

As he finally rolled into victory lane and got out of the car, he pulled the little stuffed animal out of his suit. "I finally got this monkey off my back!" he exulted. "It took twenty years, and this is the greatest win of them all. I won't say I cried on the final lap, but my eyes sure watered up."

Then he talked about his lucky penny. "All race fans are special," he said, "but a little girl who's in a wheelchair that life has not been good to, giving you a penny and wishing you luck, that's pretty special. Pretty special indeed."

The Daytona 500 win made Dale a nationwide superstar, and not just a name among NASCAR fans. He was on late-night TV talk shows. He guest starred in movies and animated TV shows.

He was as big as any rock star or athlete.

The racing world and its fans had known about him for years, but now the whole world knew the name Dale Earnhardt.

Within two years he would rank fortieth on *Forbes* magazine's list of the richest one hundred celebrities, with an income of twenty-four million dollars a year.

At the ripe old age (for a racer) of forty-seven, Dale Earnhardt had reached the pinnacle of fame.

Like Father, Like Son
1998–2000

Although he had never been more successful or famous, the rest of 1998 on the track
was a disappointment for Dale. He didn't win
another race, and he finished eighth in the
standings, well behind Jeff Gordon, who won
his third title in four years.

But 1998 was also the year that Dale
Earnhardt Jr. won his first NASCAR championship for the Dale Earnhardt, Inc. racing
team—in the Busch Series, just one level
below Winston Cup.

At twenty-four, he was far ahead of where

his father had been at the same age. Was another Earnhardt star about to take his place in the racing sky?

There had been plenty of racing dynasties—even father-son-grandson ones. In addition to the Earnhardts—Ralph, Dale, and Dale Jr.—there was Richard, Kyle, and Adam Petty. Father-son dynasties included Darrell and Michael Waltrip, the Labontes, the Jarretts, the Bodines, and the Burtons.

Dale Sr. was thrilled about his son's progress. He looked forward to the day when the two of them would appear in the same race together.

That day would not be far off.

In 1999, while winning his second straight Busch Series championship, Dale Jr. raced in five Winston Cup events for Dale Earnhardt, Inc., driving the team's second car (the first car's driver was Steve Park).

But The Intimidator wasn't going to do

Junior any special favors. When he was asked about racing against his son, he said, "On the track, he's just another competitor."

Tough talk from a tough guy, but Dale Jr. expected no less from the man who had taught him everything he knew. Anyway, it didn't bother him. Junior was a tough customer in his own right. He had learned from the master how not to be intimidated.

At a race in Michigan that year, as they drove side by side toward the checkered flag, Dale Sr. spun his son right off the track with a hard bump.

"He creamed me," Junior said afterward, but he couldn't hide the trace of a smile on his face.

Dale Sr. had a better year in 1999 than he had the year before, with an incredible tenth straight qualifier win at Daytona, a win at Bristol, and two victories at his favorite track, Talladega. But it was good enough for only

seventh place that year, only one spot higher than the year before.

Dale's injuries were still bothering him—particularly around his neck area. He decided that, if he wanted to keep racing—and he did—he needed to have off-season disc surgery.

He only hoped he could recover in time to challenge for his eighth title in 2000—his son's first full year in Winston Cup competition.

Junior was a different sort of driver than his daddy. He was smooth, careful, and calculating—more like his granddaddy Ralph, in fact. Reporters were already making comparisons, and some were saying Junior was even more talented than Dale.

That got Dale's competitive juices flowing. His son might be great someday, but he had a long way to go to catch his daddy and his grandpa.

• • •

In 2000 Junior won his first two Winston Cup races. After the second win, at Richmond (in just his sixteenth race on the circuit!), Dale came up to his son, grabbed him by the collar, and whispered, "Congratulations, son. I love you. Find your own way home."

Dale Sr. also won two races in 2000. Fully recovered from his surgery, he had signed a new four-year contract with Childress and was rounding into top form again.

He had thirteen top-five finishes, five second-place finishes, and eight straight top tens.

He ended up in second place at the end of the year, just behind winner Bobby Labonte. Those who'd said Dale Earnhardt was over the hill, that he was finished, that he could never compete for a championship again, had to eat their words.

Earnhardt might be about to turn fifty, but he was still Earnhardt.

Dale's earnings from racing for 2000 were almost five million dollars—an incredible sum when you consider what NASCAR drivers made when he started out. Dale and the sport had come up together, and both were now as big as it gets.

His victory at Talladega in October 2000 was vintage Intimidator. In an astonishing finish, at the age of forty-nine—two years older than the oldest man ever to win a Winston Cup event—he went from twenty-second position to first in the final ten laps.

It was the seventy-sixth win of Dale Earnhardt's Winston Cup career.

No one knew it then, but the amazing victory at Talladega would also be his last.

The Final Turn
2001

The year 2000, while it marked a great come-back year for Dale, had been a tough one for NASCAR. Three young drivers, including Adam Petty, son of Kyle and grandson of King Richard, had been killed on the track that year.

All of them lost their lives to the same injury—basal skull fracture—caused by the snapping back and forward of the head and neck when their car slammed into a wall or another vehicle.

That made six driver deaths in ten years. Suddenly, there was a great outcry for safer driver restraints. Dale joined in the effort, but not because he felt he himself was in danger.

He was thinking of Dale Jr.

After Adam Petty's death, he found himself avoiding Adam's father. Kyle Petty understood where Dale was coming from. So the still-grieving father was surprised on the morning of the 2001 Daytona 500, when Dale approached him, told him he loved him, and gave him a hug.

Petty burst into sobs, and Dale just kept holding him for about two minutes, until they were both okay. "Now let's go get 'em," Dale told him.

All that week—Speed Week at Daytona—Dale had seemed on top of the world. He was competitive in all of the shorter races and was looking forward to another great run at the big one—the 500.

It would mark his 651st straight race—an incredible run, and only four races short of Terry Labonte's "Iron Man" streak.

Before the race, Dale found Labonte and told him they ought to arrange a ceremony for the next month, when Dale would break the record. "We'll do a promotion if nothing happens to me before then," he told Labonte.

Those were words the older driver would never forget.

It was going to be an exciting 500. In addition to Dale, among the other drivers favored to win were his son Dale Jr. and Michael Waltrip—Darrell's son. Both were now driving for Dale Earnhardt, Inc.

Dale strapped himself into his car, then paused for his usual prayer with Teresa. It was a prayer for wisdom and safety, the same one he uttered before every race. He said, "Amen," kissed his wife, and started up his engine. It was the last time they ever saw each other.

Dale started the race in seventh position. All day long he was in the thick of things, and as the final lap approached, he was running third—right behind Michael Waltrip in first place and Dale Jr. in second.

Shielding his eyes from the blinding sun as he sped down the backstretch of the race's final lap, he could see the red-and-black DEI logo on both the leading cars.

It must have made him proud.

He had no chance to win on this day, and he knew it. Instead, he decided to run interference for his son and his teammate, blocking any other cars from coming up and challenging them for the lead in the final moments of the race.

As he watched the two lead cars head into the final turn—turn number four—Dale was not thinking of Neil Bonnett, who'd died on that very same turn in 1994. He never thought of Neil at those moments—only the race. He knew that that was how Neil would have wanted it.

Today as he approached the final turn, he looked in his rearview mirror and saw

Sterling Marlin's car coming up behind him. Instead of speeding up—his natural inclination and what he would surely have done if he'd been in a position to win the race—Dale slowed down.

Marlin's car bumped his back bumper. Dale's car went out of control, and he crashed head-on into the wall at 185 miles per hour.

Eleven seconds later, Michael Waltrip passed under the checkered flag, with Dale Jr. right behind him.

But Dale Earnhardt did not see it happen. He was already gone.

Gone forever.

For a while nobody was sure what had happened. The crash hadn't looked that bad—certainly not as bad as the one at Talladega in 1996.

But when Dale did not get out of the car and rescue workers had to start cutting open the roof, everyone's heart sank. And when they loaded him into the ambulance, and it rolled away in no particular hurry, people started to realize that the unthinkable had happened.

Dale Earnhardt—bulletproof Dale Earnhardt, the Man in Black—was dead.

His wounds were massive—eight broken ribs, a broken ankle, a fractured breastbone and collarbone, and the fatal basal skull fracture.

The racing world went into mourning.

The greatest racer of his time, if not of all time, had died in the final lap of NASCAR's greatest race, on the same turn where his best friend had been killed seven years earlier.

It was as if Michael Jordan had died on the basketball court in the last minute of the seventh game of the championship series. As if a president had been shot to death on the last day of his term.

Shock, disbelief, and sadness rolled like waves, engulfing Dale's millions of fans, and tens of millions of others who heard the news.

A larger-than-life force had met its end.

Racing would never see his likes again. "He was the last cowboy," said Kyle Petty, expressing the view of most NASCAR drivers and fans.

Dale's funeral at Calvary Church in Charlotte was attended by thirty-two hundred people. The entire NASCAR family was there, along with so many others, both great and humble, whom Dale's life had touched over the years.

But Dale's larger family—the working men and women all over the country who wore his number 3 on the backs of their jackets and painted it on their cars, who bought The Intimidator souvenirs and taught their kids to count to ten by saying, "One . . . two . . . Earnhardt . . . four . . ."—they wanted something more.

All across America, throughout 2001, the tributes poured forth. Thousands made the pilgrimage to Kannapolis, leaving flowers, poems, and bible verses behind.

They are still coming, five years later.

The week after Dale's death, NASCAR held its next Winston Cup race—and true to his daddy's legacy, Dale Jr. was behind the wheel of his red number 8 car.

Determined to win the race in his father's honor, Junior crashed horribly on the very first lap, smashing into the wall, in what looked like an instant replay of the crash that had killed his father the week before.

The crowd gasped in horror and held its collective breath—but thankfully, Junior walked away from the wreck, shaken but uninjured. "Just a little bruised up," he told reporters afterward. "We'll be okay."

All through 2001, every weekend, at every track, there were solemn tributes to the man who, more than any other, had made NASCAR racing the number one sport in the country.

Flowers everywhere. Prayers. Everyone in the stands holding a number 3 pennant and chanting his name.

Even those many fans who'd hated Dale's style of racing—the ones who'd booed him every time he bumped another car or ran some poor driver off the track—even they grieved for NASCAR's great working-class hero.

He had come from nothing, with no prospects and no education. Nothing but sheer determination, talent, and plain old bull-headedness.

And he'd conquered every mountain he climbed.

If he could do it, his legions of fans believed, so could they. He was them, and they were him.

Soon his face was on a postage stamp. Then a silver dollar. Then a monopoly board.

Even in death Dale Earnhardt continued to sell merchandise like no other figure in his sport.

Oh, the world would go on, and so would NASCAR. But neither would see the likes of Dale Earnhardt again.

For More Information

BOOKS

Mayne, Kenny. *3: The Dale Earnhardt Story*. New York: ESPN Books, 2004.

Montville, Leigh. *At the Altar of Speed: The Fast Life and Tragic Death of Dale Earnhardt*. New York: Broadway Books, 2002.

Moriarty, Frank. *Dale Earnhardt*. New York: MetroBooks, 2001.

Persinger, Kathy. *Dale Earnhardt: The Intimidator*, Champaign, IL: Sports Publishing, Inc., 2000.

Phillips, Benny, and Ben Blake, with Dale Earnhardt. *Dale Earnhardt—Determined*. Charlotte, NC: UMI Publications, 1998.

Regruth, John. *Dale Earnhardt: The Final Record.*
Osceola, WI: MBI Publishing, 2001.

Uehorn, Frank. *The Intimidator.* Asheboro, NC:
Down Home Press, 1999.

Wilkinson, Sylvia. *Dirt Tracks to Glory.* Chapel Hill,
NC: Algonquin Books, 1983.

Woods, Bob. *Pit Pass: Behind the Scenes of
NASCAR.* New York: Reader's Digest
Children's Books, 2005.

VIDEOS

Pepper, Barry. DVD. *3,* two-disc collector's edition.
DVD. Directed by Russell Mulcahy. Burbank,
CA: ESPN Original Entertainment, 2004.

WEBSITES

www.daleearnhardt.net
www.nascar.com